☆☆☆☆☆☆☆☆

Radigan Cares

☆☆☆☆☆☆☆☆

By Jeannette Eyerly

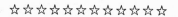

RADIGAN CARES

ESCAPE FROM NOWHERE

THE GIRL INSIDE

A GIRL LIKE ME

GRETCHEN'S HILL

THE WORLD OF ELLEN MARCH

DROP-OUT

MORE THAN A SUMMER LOVE

☆☆☆☆☆☆☆☆☆☆☆☆☆☆☆☆☆☆☆☆☆☆☆☆☆

Radigan Cares

by
Jeannette Eyerly

☆☆☆☆☆☆☆☆☆☆☆☆☆☆☆☆☆☆☆☆☆☆☆☆☆

J. B. LIPPINCOTT COMPANY
Philadelphia   ☆   New York

The time of this story is the future, and the characters and events described in it are fictitious. Cedar City is not a real city, nor is it located in a real state. Some of the states holding Presidential primaries, however, are called by name.

To the Senator
who fused logic and emotion
for a new generation

☆☆☆☆☆☆☆☆

Radigan Cares

☆☆☆☆☆☆☆☆

Chapter 1

THERE WERE TWO other guys ahead of me when I got to Steinfeld's office. I wasn't surprised to see either one. Both were hoods. Though at one time we'd been in the same room at school, nobody spoke. There was a flicker of glances all around and that was all.

I sat down in a straight-backed chair as far away from the two of them as I could get, letting my spine slide down until I found a place for my head to rest. I then folded my arms across my chest, stretched out my legs, and shut my eyes.

Almost at once, the shuffle and scuffle in the corridor outside began to fade. The sound of typewriter keys coming from the next office, like corn popping in a pan, grew fainter. Then, almost at once, instead of sitting outside Steinfeld's office, I was at the wheel of a Maserati—one was currently on display in the showroom window of Bromley Motors on High Street—traveling a cool hundred and twenty miles an hour down the River Road with a gorgeous girl at my side. I tried for the girl's face but couldn't quite

9

make it out. It wasn't anybody I knew, I decided. Certainly, it wasn't Monica Shoemaker, who I had to stop going out with ever since she'd started thinking she owned me. And it wasn't Patty Gaskell, who'd been my girl during my junior year.

Whoever this one was, she was crazy about me. She had moved as close to my side as she could get, and was letting her hands kind of riffle through my hair. "Douglas," she was saying, in this soft sexy voice, "*kiss* me."

Then someone said my name again, only this time it wasn't any girl. "Hey," I said, coming to, "what's going on here?" Steinfeld was standing in the door of his office. The two boys had left and I'd not even heard them go.

Feeling foolish, I got up and followed Steinfeld into his office. There wasn't anything to do except watch as he opened up a folder and began looking at the papers inside. There were a lot of them. There was probably stuff in there, I thought, that had been following me around since I'd started kindergarten.

Steinfeld kept on reading and I began to get uncomfortable. I wished I could see what was written there about me. Whatever it was, it was making Steinfeld anything but happy.

Still, I told myself, I didn't have anything to worry about. Otherwise Steinfeld who'd been new at school that fall, wouldn't have waited until after the beginning of second semester to send for me. Actually, ever since I'd started to junior high some guidance counselor had had me in once or twice a year for a going over, trying to discover what made me tick. But that was my business not theirs. Anyone who could get to be a senior and only flunk one course was doing all right.

10

Flunking that course, it turned out, taught me something. It showed me just how narrow the margin was between passing and flunking. It took a bit of doing to make it right down the line with a card full of C's, a D-plus or two, and when I slipped too much, a D. Although I envied Curley Matthews' remark that he was living a life of "E's," I wouldn't have wanted Curley's record. He had also dropped out of school and I had no intention of doing that. It was my plan to graduate—that would get my folks off my neck —then let the draft get me. Not because I believed in all that crap about serving your country, but because I didn't want to go to jail. After I got out of the army, or maybe the marines, I planned to go to South America or somewhere and seek my fortune. With my grades there wasn't a chance that any college would have me, which would be a break for my folks. My brother Norm was going to college and a fat lot of satisfaction they were getting out of *him*. Norm spent most of his time marching around carrying protest signs or being carried away from campus gatherings by the police.

I jerked to attention as Steinfeld closed the folder and snapped a question that seemed to read my mind. "Just what *are* your plans, Radigan, for the future?"

"My plans, sir?" I was so startled that I groped.

Steinfeld smiled, not unpleasantly, and I gave him back one as good as I'd received. "Well, sir,"—saying "sir," I'd discovered, always helped to create a good impression when one was needed—"I haven't any plans, in particular. At least, none of my making—though I seem to remember that Uncle Sam has something in mind for me not long after I graduate."

"You're planning on graduating?"

"Sir?"

I guess I must have sounded pretty alarmed, for Steinfeld grinned. "I'm not saying you won't graduate, but the picture isn't all one of rejoicing." He took some more papers from the folder. "Listen to these reports. 'Fifty percent chance of failing course,' 'not a bad kid, but lazy,' 'behind on all written work,' 'barely passing.' Well?"

I was getting hot. "It doesn't sound too good, does it?"

"No, it doesn't. And I'd like to know why."

"Why?"

"That's right. Why. If we're to believe the scores on the standard intelligence tests you've been taking since you started to school, you're not stupid. Yet four out of your five teachers indicate that you're in serious trouble."

I shot Steinfeld a swift look, wondering if I could level with him. What would he think if I did try to explain? About my brother, Norm, for instance. Norm wanted to overturn the Government. Not because he wanted to replace it with anything in particular, but because he thought society was rotten. Or explain about my dad, who was at the opposite end of the pole from Norm. My dad spent Monday through Friday on the road selling pharmaceutical supplies and Saturday and Sunday "improving" either himself or "the property." My mother wasn't quite so easy to figure out, but as soon as Norm and I were both in school all day she went back to her old job of clerking in Biggers' department store. And just what had hard work got either one of them? For that matter, where had working all day with a bunch of punk kids got Steinfeld?

The answer to both questions was, of course, "nowhere at all." And that was why I couldn't swallow Norm's line

12

of talk or settle for the kind of world my folks had. I was outside both of them, and that was where I had planned to stay.

"Yes?"

Steinfeld's voice was edgy and it brought me back with a jerk. "Maybe I'd better try a little harder. Sir."

"Maybe you had," Steinfeld said.

He was finished with me. I got up and went out.

Outside, I braced myself against the wind. It had grown colder since morning—February is just about the most miserable month of the year—and when I passed the section of the parking lot reserved for teachers, I could hear somebody grinding the starter of his car. As I came nearer, I saw it was Watt Tyler, my American Government teacher. I wondered if he was the one who had knifed me with "not a bad kid, but lazy" or the one who'd written that I had a fifty percent chance of passing the course. On the other hand, American Government might be the one class in which I *wasn't* in trouble. In any case, I decided, I couldn't afford to take any chances. If Tyler was on my side, I wanted to help him. If he wasn't, helping him get his car started would do more good than harm.

The Rrrrrrrr of the starter was growing fainter as I put my head in the half-opened window of Tyler's car. "I'm afraid you're just running down your battery, Mr. Tyler. Then that car's never going to start."

"I suppose so. The internal combustion engine is something that I have never pretended to understand. What should I do?"

Maybe Tyler throwing himself on my mercy like he did, brought out the best. I don't know. But in any case, observing

13

Tyler at close range—in class, I sat in the last seat in the last row, just as far away from the firing line as I could get—I could see how young he really was. He didn't look much older than my brother Norm, who's twenty-two. But he would have to be older. Some.

"If I get my car behind you and give you a push," I said, "maybe we might get yours started."

"Your car will start?"

"The Blue Bomb always starts."

Mr. Tyler said, "Oh," a little doubtfully and, in truth, I thought as I headed toward my car, I couldn't blame him. But in spite of its advanced age and appearance, it *did* always start. At least, until now it always had. I stepped on the starter with a kind of rotary motion that The Bomb responds to, delicately adjusted the choke, then tried again— aware that fifty feet away Mr. Tyler, his breath steaming in the cold, was watching me.

"Come on, Bomb Baby," I whispered. "Come on!"

Then, as if it had really heard me, the engine turned over and caught. I let the car sit there, quivering like a race-horse at the post, until I was sure the motor wouldn't die on me, then maneuvered around until I was behind Mr. Tyler's car. Then I stuck my head out the window and yelled instructions. But nothing happened, though bumper to bumper I pushed Mr. Tyler's car from one end of the parking lot to the other and back again.

I got out of my car and walked up to the window of his. "I'm sorry but I'm afraid it's no go. But I can push you to a service station, if you want."

"I'd be grateful, Doug, if you did. And even more grateful if you'd do an errand for me. Deliver those boxes there

14

in the back seat to the Kieran headquarters. It's important that they get down there this afternoon."

As he spoke, Watt Tyler fumbled a billfold out of an inside pocket.

It wasn't a fat billfold, I noticed, either with credit cards or money. And though my own wallet wasn't any fatter, I shook my head before teach could take out a bill.

"You needn't pay me. I'll be glad to deliver the stuff," I said, careful not to overdo the All-American boy bit. Whatever Watt Tyler was, he wasn't dumb. "Where did you say you want the boxes delivered?"

"Kieran headquarters. It's between Eighth and Ninth Streets on Oak Avenue, the south side of the street. It's a hole in the wall, but it's the best we can afford until some money comes rolling in."

I said, "Right-o," and began taking the boxes out of Tyler's car and putting them in The Bomb. I might not know who Kieran was, or what he was running for, but I could find his headquarters. I was sure of that.

Kieran headquarters turned out to be a hole in the wall, just like Watt Tyler said it was. But I couldn't have missed it. Red, white, and blue bunting was draped around all over everywhere in the window, along with a bunch of posters, bumper and window stickers all reading "Kieran Cares." A "Kieran for President" sign was above the door. For President. So that was it. I remembered reading something about this senator who'd come out of nowhere and was seeking his party's nomination. Until then it had been up for grabs between ex-Senator Swallow, who'd barely lost the nomination four years before, and Governor Frazier who'd won it only to be defeated in the general election. You

15

couldn't turn on the boob tube without seeing one or the other of them. And I was almost as sick of Frazier, who talked out of both sides of his mouth at once, as I was of Swallow who thought everything would be all right with the country if we shipped all the blacks back to Africa.

A car that might have been a blood brother of The Bomb pulled out of a parking place just as I drove up, and I slid neatly into it. Moreover, there were almost fifteen minutes left on the parking meter. That would give me time to carry the boxes inside without having to put a dime of my own in the slot.

As I approached the building, my arms full of boxes, a young man with a reddish beard and a pipe in his hand opened the door for me.

"I don't know what you've got there," he said, "but you can put it down here."

"I don't know what I've got either," I said, "but I'm delivering it for Watt Tyler. There's more of it outside."

The young man with the pipe turned to a boy sitting at a card table pecking at a typewriter. "Let that list go for a minute, will you, Joe, and give our friend here a hand?"

The boy, who looked younger than me, said, "Sure, boss," and after we'd carried the boxes in and stacked them in a corner, I looked around. A half dozen kids sat at an improvised counter that ran the length of the room. What they were doing I couldn't tell, but they were sure busy at it. An older woman at a nearby desk was talking on the telephone. A girl, with long oily hair, was running off letters on a duplicating machine and a half dozen other people, mostly young, were sitting around a long table addressing envelopes. There were so many empty soft-drink bottles, and paper cups half-filled with coffee sitting around, there was scarcely room for the work that was going on. Waste paper spilled out of wastebaskets and overflowed from cardboard cartons. At the far end of the room, where some flimsy-looking partitions had been put up to form a couple of offices, boxes of fresh supplies were stacked halfway to the ceiling.

The young man with the beard and the pipe, who'd opened the door for me when I came in, read my mind. "It is a mess, but we get things done. If you'd like to help, we can always use an extra pair of hands. Or legs. Or, better yet, a car. A lot of the kids aren't old enough to have a driver's license yet. But that's one thing about our man, Kieran. He gets 'em of all ages."

I shook my head. Even if politics was something in which I was interested—which I was not—anybody with half an eye could see that they were working for a lost cause. "Sorry," I said. "I'm pretty busy right now."

Then I saw her. Standing in the door of one of the "offices" at the end of the room. At first glance, she wasn't my type of girl at all. Pale, blonde hair pulled back and tied with a stringy scarf. Big, black glasses and a shaggy gray sweater two sizes too big for her. Corduroy pants tucked into the top of beat-up suede boots.

Then I took another look. In spite of everything she'd done to herself, I recognized her. She was a dead-image of the girl I'd dreamed sat beside me as I'd traveled a hundred and twenty miles an hour in my Maserati down the River Road.

17

★ ★ ★ ★ ★ ★ ★

Chapter 2

☆ ☆ ☆ ☆ ☆ ☆ ☆

ALTHOUGH TRAFFIC ON the way home was so heavy that at times The Bomb didn't move at all, I couldn't help grinning. The Girl—I had to call her that until I found out her name—had done her darnedest to cover up her looks, but she couldn't fool me. Even by skinning back her hair like that. It was really blonde. Not just hair-colored hair that had been bleached out until it looked like straw. Even the glasses were a put-on. If she was half-blind, nobody but nobody, would wear frames like that.

Once off the clogged avenue that led from town and onto the freeway, I had to stop thinking about her. Then driving took all my attention. Though there are plenty of scratches and dents on The Bomb, there's not a one I put there and as far as I know I've never put a scratch or a dent on anybody else's car either. So I'm careful. Although The Bomb might not look like much compared with all the other cars moving along the four-lane highway at an even sixty-mile-an-hour clip, she could keep up with them and still have power to spare.

As I approached the exit nearest my street, I toyed with

the idea of *not* turning off. It wasn't a new idea. I mean, the idea of staying on the freeway until it reached the Interstate and then just to keep on going west.

The only trouble was going on would take money—at least, more money than I had. It was, in fact, going to take some pretty careful management to make the money I'd earned at the cement plant the summer before last until June. My plan, then, was to get another job and work at that until the draft caught up with me. Ever since I'd turned sixteen and got a work permit, I'd decided it was bad enough going to school, without going to school *and* working.

I took the exit at the posted speed of thirty and turned north at the bridge over the freeway into Paradise Acres.

The Miracle Realty Company advertised it every Sunday on TV. While the announcer was going on about "living in Paradise," pictures of split-levels, ranch houses, and what they described as "colonials" flitted across the screen.

My folks had bought a house in Paradise Acres three years ago—a split level. There were so many other houses like it on our street you could have wound up in the wrong bed if you didn't know exactly where you were going. It was for this house that my mother had gone back to work. It was for this house that my dad frequently stayed out an extra day on his territory. This house was their most prized possession. And now it possessed *them*. The play on words that I'd made just sort of unintentionally pleased me.

As I turned in the drive I noticed that the lights were on, which meant, most likely, that my mother had caught a ride with somebody instead of taking the bus home as she usually had to do.

19

I drove around to the back of the house and parked the car on the cement apron my dad had built at the side of the garage especially for The Bomb. My dad was always building something, like in the winter, finishing off a place in the attic so Norm and I could have a "study." What a laugh! Nobody studied around our house. When Norm was home he was always down in the basement lettering posters to carry in some march or other. And I studied less than practically anybody I knew.

If, in the winter, my dad wasn't building something, he had his nose in some seed catalog or was inching his way through the Self-Improvement Course he was taking from somebody's correspondence school. He spent his summers digging, fertilizing, and spraying. Our grass was the greenest and the thickest on the block. The summer before my dad had entered the Rose Show—how Norm had carried on over that—and had won a red ribbon for some rose called "Dainty Bess."

If my father didn't understand me, I didn't understand him and that just about canceled the score. Some people, though, do say we look alike; I don't see it. He's not as tall as I am and his hair, what he's got left, is dark brown instead of reddish like mine.

As I came in the back door and into the kitchen, my mother called out, "Doug, is that you?"

For about the fraction of a second, I debated not answering at all—or saying that "No, it was Lord Snowdon, or Dickie Smothers." But I didn't. I said it was me, all right.

"Oh, I'm glad," my mother said, coming into the kitchen. "Your father's home early—he's upstairs showering now—and if Normie should decide to come home—last weekend he said he might—we'd all be here together."

20

My mother is always making remarks like that. Wishing we could all be together, apparently forgetting that when we are the evening usually ends with her bawling, my father losing his temper, and Norm, laughing disagreeably, going off to bed, and me leaving to ride around in The Bomb until things cool off.

I opened a bag of potato chips on the counter and took a handful. "Even if Norm should come home, I'm not going to be here."

"A girl?" my mother said. "Monica?" She looked hopeful. Of all the girls I've ever gone out with, she liked Monica the best. I shook my head; an idea had just come to me. Why not whip down to Kieran headquarters after dinner—that afternoon I'd heard someone say the place would be open until nine—get acquainted with my new little friend and drive her home? "Somebody new."

My mother said, "Oh," in a disappointed way, then she laughed. She has rather a good laugh, not put-on at all. "You and your girls! What's this one's name?"

"Ask me tomorrow."

"I don't see how you can go out with a girl when you don't know her name."

I said, "Easy," and taking the bag of potato chips with me faded out of the kitchen.

When I left home a little after seven thirty, Norm still hadn't arrived. So far, that was the only good thing about the evening, my father having spent the entire time we were eating on the subject of getting me into college. He's got a lot of hang-ups, but this college thing is the worst of all.

If he'd waited until dessert, even, but no. Right along with the first bite of pot roast and browned potatoes he clears his throat and says that this past week he'd been

21

making inquiries about some *smaller* schools, and that one of his customers had told him about a junior college in the northern part of the state that was *looking* for students.

"A *junior* college," says my mother. *"That's interesting."* She gives my ankle a jab under the table, but when I don't say anything my father picks up a folder lying beside his place and reads, "Merryside! This small, inter-denominational liberal arts college, situated in the thriving community of Thorpse, surrounded by acres of rolling farmland, caters to the *whole* student."

This time my mother didn't say anything and I didn't even look up. I didn't think my father needed any encouragement to go on, and he didn't.

"I daresay it doesn't sound good to *you,* but whether it appeals to you or not isn't the question." His voice was edgy. "The point is they are looking for students, and in your case going to Merryside would be better than not going at all. . . ."

I said, "Better for who?"

My mother said, "Douglas, please. Not to your father! Besides, dear, I think it's 'whom.' "

My father got white around the mouth the way he does when he's trying not to lose his temper because the doctor says it's bad for him and pushed his plate back. I mumbled something about being sorry—I don't want my dad having a heart attack on my account—and he pulled his plate back and started in again on good old Merryside.

As soon as I'd finished eating, I excused myself. My mother said, "Don't be late," and my father said, "Be careful," which is what they've both been saying ever since I got The Bomb and started going off by myself.

22

Actually, I'd been a little hot myself at dinner. No guy, or I suppose for that matter, no girl wants somebody else mapping out their lives for them, but as soon as I started driving, I cooled off. The Bomb always does that for me.

Instead of getting on the freeway to go downtown, I took the long way driving past school. Not to look at the school, but because the Pizza Hut, Rubin's Delicatessen, Brownie's Drug, and Pinky's Pastry Parlor where they sell all the ice cream slop girls like to eat, is just across the street from it. Kids call it The Strip.

It was still too early in the evening for much to be going on, but even so and in spite of the fact that it was pretty cold, a bunch of guys were milling around on the sidewalk. Cars came and went, their exhausts making big puffballs of vapor. Even with the windows of The Bomb rolled up, you could smell the gas in the air.

I was driving around the island that separates the stores from the street, looking for anybody I could kill time with when I spotted Curley Matthews. I would have joined him if I hadn't noticed he was with the same guys I'd see in Steinfeld's office that afternoon. Curley himself isn't any prize, but either of the other two mean possible trouble and the three of them together guaranteed it. In fact, someone had already smeared red paint and "Rubin is a Jew bastard" on the window of the delicatessen which is next door to the Pastry Shop and my guess was that it was Curley. He hated Rubin almost as much as he hated "Shadow" Morrison, the cop, who patrolled The Strip.

Though it might not have been Curley. Earlier in the fall, Rubin had got in trouble with some other Greeley High kids. One afternoon when twenty-five or thirty of them

23

moved into the delicatessen and started swiping gum, candy bars, and boxes of cookies and stuff from the shelves Rubin, instead of pretending he didn't see the kids take it the way he usually did, called the cops. Somebody overheard Rubin make the call and by the time the squad car got there the kids had scattered. So, though nobody got picked up, the kids had it in for Rubin.

As it happened, Curley and I had been in the deli only a couple of afternoons before and I swiped a handful of Mars bars while Curley paid for a couple of cold Cokes at the check-out counter. That was different, though, from cleaning out the place.

I drove on, though it was still too early to go down to Kieran headquarters. If I got there much before closing time they'd probably put me to work. And I wanted no part of that.

But I did notice that the gas gauge registered less than a quarter full. Although that would be plenty for ordinary circumstances, I couldn't help thinking that the circumstances that night might be *extra*ordinary. The Girl might like to take a little drive before going home. She might even like to drive out to Smitty's Place, going the long way, on the River Road.

There weren't any other cars at the pumps when I turned into Smiley's Service Station. Through the windows I could see Pete Quigley studying. Quig is about the only square guy I really like. He and I had spent a lot of time together. Summers, we'd explored almost every inch of the big woods on the other side of City Park. We'd gone swimming and played sandlot baseball. Practically every Saturday all winter we'd gone to the Strand, a movie house that played only

24

Westerns, horror films, or ones about outer space. We'd buy a big bag of popcorn and sit through the show twice, and come groggily out into the fading daylight and then take our separate buses for home.

But Quig's father dying had changed all that. Quig, who'd turned sixteen just a week before I did, got a job after school pumping gas at Smiley's, and all day Saturday he worked as a carry-out boy at a supermarket. And, of course, summers no longer counted because I was working full time. Whatever in-between time remained, he studied. He had to. Since his father's death he had to go to college via the scholarship route or not at all. Even so, although we didn't see each other much we were still friends. I would have done almost anything for Quig, and I know he would do the same for me.

I pressed the horn on The Bomb in the rhythm pattern that Quig recognized and watched as he shrugged into an old sheep-lined jacket and pulled a stocking cap down over his ears. He was grinning as he came up to the car.

"Fill it up, sir? With premium, of course."

"Pretty funny," I said. "Three gallons. Regular. And make it snappy, son. I've got a date."

By the time Quig had gone around to the rear of the car and removed the cap from the gas tank, I was back there, too, watching as Quig fitted the nozzle of the gas pump into the tank.

It wasn't the first time I'd noticed Quig's hands. They were even bigger than mine, which is saying something, and yet they were kind of delicate, too. They looked the way an artist's hands should look. That's what he wanted to be, an artist. He'd settled on architecture, though, as a

25

better way of making a living. There were a couple of younger girl Quigleys and a kid brother that Quig was going to have to put through college, too.

Quig had put the cap back on the tank. "Check your oil, sir? The pressure in your tires? Perhaps you need a new pair of blades in those windshield wipers?"

I shook my head, tired of the game. "Just the gas." I glanced at the figure on the pump, took a crumpled dollar bill from my pocket and added the necessary change. "Everything going OK?"

Quig didn't answer for a minute, then said, "Sure. Great!"

"It was great you got elected to the Student Council," I said, glad that at last I'd remembered to mention it. I *had* forgotten to vote—though I'd intended to when early last fall I heard that Quig was running. As it turned out, he'd got elected without me, though not by very many votes.

Quig grinned. "Yeah. I'm glad I made it, though, so far, I'm just a lone voice crying in the wilderness. One guy hasn't got much chance against the establishment." He paused, cocking an ear toward the station. "There's the phone. Too bad. Something I wanted to show you, but tomorrow will do as well. See you."

I waited for a stream of cars to pass then moved into the traffic pattern. Talking to Quig had depressed me. Life, if you thought about it—which I tried hard not to do—really screwed things up. Why did Quig's father have to die? And why did my father and mother, who would have given almost anything in the world to have a kid like Quig for their son, get somebody like Norm and me?

In disgust, I snapped on the radio and kept switching stations until I found something I liked. Something cheerful, with a good beat. I needed it. It had just occurred to me that after I made the trip to Kieran headquarters, The Girl might not be there. Then to burn me even more, a police car followed me all the way downtown. Even before I got a look at the face of the cop driving, I knew it was "The Shadow." Some kids call him worse than that. He hates us, and we hate him—though, as I said, nobody worse than Curley Matthews who "Shad" had had it in for ever since he caught Curley swiping a hubcap off a police car.

I got out and peered through the window of the headquarters. Between the posters and strips of bunting hanging around, I could see that there was still plenty going on. The young man with the reddish beard and the pipe was still there. So was the boy called Joe, who'd helped me carry in Watt Tyler's boxes that afternoon. Three kids sat at the improvised counter putting rubber bands around stacks of yellow cards and filing them in shoe boxes.

I saw The Girl last of all. By herself, as alone as if she was on a desert island, she sat at a typewriter at a desk in the very back of the room. Although she was still wearing those nutty glasses, a few pieces of hair had managed to get loose so she looked even prettier than before.

I went inside.

Red Beard waved his pipe when he saw me. "Welcome aboard. I was hoping someone would show up to sweep out the place. Twelve hours in this place, even for a loyal Kieran supporter, is too much. Broom and dustpan's there in the back room."

I looked around to see if the guy was talking to somebody else but there wasn't anybody there but me.

"There's some boxes in the back room, too," he added,

27

"and you can leave it all in the alley behind the building."
He got up as he spoke and yawning took his coat from a
nail pounded in the plasterboard wall behind him. "Well,
good night everybody. See you tomorrow. Last fellow out
leave the key at the filling station across the street."

I looked after him as he went out, then returned to Joe.
"What's *that* all about?"

Joe laughed. "No mystery. Gabby, our fearless leader,
wants you to sweep out. Like he said."

For a minute I thought I was going to blow, then suddenly it struck me funny. "Man, you've got me wrong.
I didn't come here to work. I came to see a girl." I jerked
my head toward the back of the room. "Give her a break
and drive her home."

"Emily? You mean, drive Emily home?"

This time, Joe laughed even louder and though I felt
myself getting hot again, I had to cool it. Joe was too small
to fight—a half head shorter than me and at least twenty
pounds lighter—even if I'd wanted to. And besides, who
could take a poke at anyone with a face like a good-natured
baby. Besides, I decided that I liked the name of Emily.
"Yeah," I said. "Drive her home. Anything wrong with
that?"

Joe shook his head. "Not a thing. It's just that you're
not the only guy who's had the same idea. Gabby, for instance."

"Gabby? The guy with the beard?" I laughed, not be-
lieving it. "He's too old for her, in any case."

"Maybe. I've got somebody of my own that suits me
just fine, so I haven't tried. Hey, Molly! Come on over. I
want you to meet a new recruit."

28

I grinned as a cute, black-haired little girl got up from the counter where she'd been working.

"Molly Greenaway, meet . . ."

"Doug Radigan."

Molly put out her hand. "Hi! You're still in school?"

I took it as a compliment. "Greeley High. Graduate in June."

"Joe and I go to Washington High," Molly said. "But we're only miserable juniors."

"Nothing wrong with juniors that a couple of years won't cure," Joe put in. "Maybe by the time we graduate, eighteen-year-olds will have the vote."

"Yay! Kieran!" Molly said, making like a cheerleader.

"In the meantime, I'll drive you home," Joe said. "Round up your gang."

As Joe spoke, the two girls who'd been working with Molly pushed back their chairs and chattering put on their coats. Only seconds later the four of them were gone.

I looked down the long cluttered room where The Girl sat, still typing, then slowly began walking toward her. In spite of what Joe had said about nobody getting to first base with her, I wasn't nervous. I couldn't remember a girl who hadn't gone out with me when I asked her.

Not until I got even with her desk, did she look up. And even then she didn't seem to see me. She took off the glasses, squeezed her eyes tightly shut, then opened them. "Tired." Her tone was vague and a little apologetic.

And she *was* tired. I could see that. There were faint bluish smudges beneath her eyes and they made her eyes bluer than any I'd ever seen. And she was young. Seventeen . . . eighteen. Not more than nineteen at the most. But

29

however old she was, she was too young for Red Beard. The knowledge made me feel even more secure and confident.

"My name's Doug Radigan." I sat down on the corner of her desk, letting one leg swing.

"Should I know you?" She looked puzzled.

I favored her with my most dazzling smile. "Why, yes. *I* think so, anyway. And I'd like to know *you.*"

She smiled at that so I knew things were going all right. A minute later she stuck out her hand. Although it looked soft, she had a good firm grip. "My name is Emily Marlow. I guess we haven't met, but I'm glad you came. At this hour of the day things seem to reach a new low." Her glance took in the dozens of empty paper cups and soft-drink bottles that were sitting around everywhere, bulging wastebaskets and litter on the floor.

Maybe it was the way she looked at me when she said it, I don't know. I do know that about the next second I heard myself saying that I'd be glad to sweep out.

For that, I got a real smile. And while Emily emptied ash trays and gathered up Coke bottles and paper cups, I dumped the contents of all the wastebaskets into a big empty carton I found in the back room, and carried it out to the alley the way Red Beard had told me to do. When I came back, Emily had her coat on. A pouch purse on a long strap was slung over one shoulder and she carried a shoe box full of stamped addressed letters under one arm.

I was so startled I laughed. "Hey!" I said. "We're not through yet. And when we do go, I'm going with you."

Emily shook her head. "Thanks, Doug. But after being inside all day, I like to walk. It isn't far."

"But I counted on it. That's why I . . . I mean, I wouldn't

30

have . . ." Although I knew it was childish, I kicked at the pile of rubbish at my feet.

"That's hardly my fault, is it?"

"I guess not." I didn't know what else to say.

"Good!" She was smiling again. "I'm glad we've got that settled." She gave me a "that's a good boy" look and with a brisk "good night" opened the door to a blast of cold air.

Pennants, posters, and bunting in the window rustled and scraps of paper skittered across the floor as the door closed. A second later it opened again. "Oh, and don't forget to leave the key at the filling station across the street," she said brightly and with that was gone for good.

For about five minutes I just stood there, thinking how I'd been conned by a pretty face disguised as a . . . I couldn't find any words to express it. Monica, with all her faults, had never treated me like this.

It would serve Emily right if I walked out, leaving the place a mess. For the second time that night, I kicked at the pile of rubbish then picking up the broom I'd dropped, started sweeping.

★ ★ ★ ★ ★ ★ ★

Chapter 3

☆ ☆ ☆ ☆ ☆ ☆ ☆

I'D BEEN SORE as blazes when I delivered the key to the filling station across the street, and I was still sore when I turned into Dugan's Drive-In for a hamburger and a Coke.

The place was crowded. Outside, the cars were parked almost solid, nosing in like sardines in a can, around the brightly lighted diner. Inside, there were thirty or forty kids milling and jostling around and as many waiting to *get* in. The whole thing reminded me of a rerun of an old Mickey Mouse cartoon that I'd seen at the Galaxy the week before.

I drove around the parking area a couple of times before a space opened up, right next to Curley Matthews' Dodge. One thing about Curley's car, you can recognize it anywhere. Not only is it a diesel, but it's painted with psychedelic stripes in every color you ever saw and a few besides. Curley, who was in his car, was staring straight ahead into the diner, but turned when he heard The Bomb arrive.

Before I had turned the motor off, Curley had come over and stuck his head through the window that I rolled down for him.

32

Curley wore his hair long and it was as straight as if he ironed it. And for all I know, maybe he did.

He jerked his head toward the diner. "I think I've got a good thing going in there, if I can read the signs. In fact, *two* good things. One of which I'm willing to share with a friend." He grinned. "Interested?"

"Why not?" I said. "You don't see a beautiful blonde beside me on the seat, do you?"

Curley pretended to inspect the front seat. "Not exactly. But there is a beautiful blonde in the diner there. Lucky for you, it's the girl who's with her, the redhead, that I'm hot for. I happen to know, however, that this one chick doesn't go without the other." He turned and stared toward the diner. "If that fat guy in the green turtleneck would move out of the way you could see them both."

"Yeah," I said. "I see them." Somehow, I'd expected something better, though that was a pretty stupid expectation. Together Curley and I had been out with some almost as bad.

The light from the big floods that rimmed the parking area made the place as light as day. As the girls came closer, I could see that the blonde one wasn't really blonde at all, that she was wearing lavender lipstick, and that her eyelashes seemed to be made out of fur. The redhead, if anything, was worse. But that was Curley's problem, not mine, and he didn't seem to mind. He draped an arm around her shoulder as soon as she and the blonde had reached my car.

With an exaggerated wink in my direction, he said, "Well, now that we're all here, what say we get going? Sherlie Lou and I can take the back of The Bomb here, and you and . . ."

"Dorene Kay."

The blonde supplied her name with a little smirk and Curley picked it up. "You and Dorene Kay can do the driving."

I shook my head. "Not tonight." The words had come out without me even thinking what I was going to say.

"What do you mean, 'not tonight'?" Curley said. Already he was busy. One hand was on the door, and the other he'd worked in under the redhead's coat.

"I mean you're going in your car. I'm not going."

"But you've got to!" Curley howled.

"You're darned right." The blonde tossed her head, glared in Curley's direction. "If he don't go, if we don't each of us have a guy, then neither one of us goes. Right?"

"Right! These two guys aren't the only fish in the sea. Come on, Dorene. Let's get out of here right now."

The two of them took off across the lot, twitching their behinds between the parked cars. Curley, looking ugly, said something unprintable about what he was going to do to me the next time he saw me and then started after the girls, saying that he'd take care of everything.

After that, I cruised around for a while but I didn't see anybody I knew and about midnight I went home. The whole lousy evening from start to finish had been such a flop that I didn't see how one more thing could happen. But it did. As I went down the hall past my parents' bedroom, my mother said, "Dougie, is that you?" When I said it was, she added, "Normie's here, too. I just felt it in my bones that he was coming home."

The next morning I slept late, like I always do on Saturdays if I can, and when I came downstairs I found Norm in the kitchen eating breakfast. His plate was covered with food and he was forking it in as if it was his last meal on earth. I don't know what Norm eats at school, but at home he eats like an ox.

As I came in the room, my mother was saying, "If you'd like another egg, Normie, I'd be glad to fry it for you. You *are* thin."

I couldn't tell whether Norm was thin or not. He has this beard which is very thick and bushy, and as his hair is likewise, about all you could see of his face were his eyes and about an inch of cheek. He also was wearing a lot of different layers of clothes which tended to conceal his shape. That morning I could see that on top of his flannel shirt he had a sweater, and on top of that a dirty suede jacket with a lot of fringe dangling from it.

While Mom fixed my breakfast, she fried Norm another egg, too, and when he finally came up for air she said, *"Now,* Normie, you can speak to your brother."

Norm said he had spoken to me, which was true, I suppose, if you call a grunt speaking. But Mom let that part of it pass. After about a minute she took a deep breath and said, "I also think it would be nice, Norman, if you went downstairs and had a little visit with your father."

Under his breath, Norman said, "Oh, God!" then after scowling at his empty plate for a while, said warningly, "If I do, you know it means trouble."

"Not unless you make it mean trouble," my mother plowed right ahead, her trouble being that she never knows when to stop. "You and your father certainly ought to be able to talk about something pleasant. Bluebird houses, for instance. Right now, he's making bluebird houses for the yard next summer."

35

From Norm's reaction, my mother might as well have said that my father was in the basement making atom bombs. He leaped up from the table and started pacing around the kitchen, stopping every once and a while to clench his fists and look up at the ceiling. "My father is making bluebird houses while one third of the world's population is starving."

My mother backed off a little. "It's not *my* fault, dear."

"Oh, but that's where you're wrong!" Norm cried in a voice so loud and intense that my mother jumped again.

"Now, I don't mean you, personally," Norm said, still intense but not so loud. He jabbed a finger in her direction. "I mean that you, as a representative of a capitalistic society, are responsible."

All of a sudden, my mother laughed. "Me?" she said, in this tiny voice. There is this thing about her, she does have a pretty good sense of humor. *"Me?"*

The way she said it made me laugh. The idea of my mother, puddling around in the kitchen in a housecoat and with her hair up in curlers, being a representative of the capitalistic system, really was a gas.

Then Norm, though it killed him to do it, allowed himself this faint sort of smile. "I'm speaking figuratively, of course. But until you, me, Doug here, *everybody* becomes an activist, is willing to use force to achieve what he believes in . . ." Norm broke off when I got up from the table. "Hey," he said. "Where are you going? I haven't finished yet."

"I know," I said. "But I have." I grinned in the direction of my mother. "Good breakfast, Ma. What did Dad do with the morning paper?"

"It's in by the TV, I think," my mother said and Norm, in his most insulting manner, added, "What's *he* want with the morning paper? He doesn't read anything but the sport section."

My mother let that pass and I wandered into the living room and got the paper. First, I read the sport pages, then I leafed through the rest of the paper looking to see if there happened to be any stories about Gregory Kieran. Having swept out his local headquarters the night before, I thought I'd at least like to know what the guy stood for. The trouble was that I couldn't ask anybody without displaying my ignorance. Halfway through the paper I found a story about five or six inches long saying that Senator Gregory Kieran who, contrary to all predictions had won primary contests in both New Hampshire and Pennsylvania, was now making a strong bid in Wisconsin. I'd hoped there'd be a picture of him, too, and there was. But it only showed the back of his head and the blurry faces of a lot of kids filling a university auditorium. Not that I cared what he looked like. If I'd cared, I told myself, I would have looked at some of the pictures of him plastered all over the walls of headquarters. But I hadn't even bothered to do that.

A little later, when I went out to start The Bomb and heard loud voices and a lot of swearing coming up from the basement, I knew that my mother was having her wish. Norm was having a "visit" with my father.

By Monday, I'd decided to give Emily another chance. When I compared her to Dorene Kay, or whatever her name was, how could I do anything else? Both Dorene and her friend were too cheap even to be on a bargain counter.

I couldn't help whistling as I stowed my stuff in my locker after lunch and started off for my class in American Government. I only had about two minutes, but that was time enough. There certainly wasn't any point in getting there early. Even after the buzzer had sounded and the period started, kids would still be hanging around Watt Tyler's desk polishing the apple.

Even so, I would have made it on time if I hadn't bumped into Quig. He was carrying a pink slip in one hand, which meant that he was out of class legally, and under his arm a big, flat parcel wrapped up in brown paper.

"Hey!" Quig said. "I don't suppose you've got a minute to see a drawing, do you? I would have showed it to you last night if the phone hadn't rung when it did."

The buzzer sounded just then, so I shook my head. "I'm late right now."

"After school, then, in the journalism room?"

"I'll have to check with my secretary," I said, "but if I'm free, I'll be there." With that, I took off on the double for my class.

By the time I got there everybody was in his seat and Mr. Tyler, who was writing something on the blackboard, resisted the temptation to make a crack about me being late, for which I was grateful. Maybe that was the reason I got sort of halfway interested in what he was saying which was that for the rest of the semester we weren't going to use our textbook on American Government any more, but were going to read the newspaper every day and paperback books. He'd been writing the list on the blackboard when I came in. *The Kerner Report, Crisis in Black and White* by Silverman, *Manchild in the Promised Land* by Brown, and *Black Rage*, written by a couple of black psychiatrists.

Then he started saying that we were living through history at that very moment and that we couldn't properly study American Government without understanding the black man.

After that, my mind began to wander. Not because I had anything against the blacks but because I've never happened to know any. Norm has some friends who are Black Panthers but since their revolutionary philosophy begins where his leaves off, he once told me rather proudly, I can see why he's never brought them home. As far as Greeley High School is concerned, I don't suppose there are more than four or five black kids in the whole school.

I sort of dozed off during English, although I don't think Miss Beckman noticed, and if she did I couldn't help it. It wasn't so bad when were were reading *Catcher in the Rye* —though I personally thought Holden Caulfield was kind of a nut—but Shakespeare I didn't dig at all. Last period I bequeathed my body to gym class—there, at least, was some action—and that was school for the day.

When I got to the journalism room, Quig wasn't there yet but Monica was. I'd forgotten she did something or other on the school paper and might be around. The minute she saw me, she came twitching over.

"Douglas!" she said, "What are *you* doing here? A strong anti-establishment type like you?"

Under my breath, I said something I shouldn't have and moved across to meet Quig who'd just come in the door at the far end of the room along with a couple of other kids.

"Maybe this isn't a good place after all," Quig said. "They must be having a *Tatler* staff meeting. Let's try the library. Nobody'll be there, and I don't want anybody to get wind of this just yet."

He was right about the library. The only person there was Miss Heathrow, the librarian, who was shuffling books around on one of the shelves.

Quig laid his parcel on the table and started unwrapping it. "This is the drawing for the cover of the yearbook. Usually, it's a bunch of nothing. Last year, remember, was a drawing of a Social-type girl and Social-type boy wearing Greeley sweaters and walking hand in hand into the setting sun. Yuck." He pretended to gag, then went on. "But *my* drawing is satiric. I want it to say something. Look at this."

Even before I looked at the drawing closely, I started to grin. It was a picture of a crumbling castle with the words Horace Greeley High over the door. A couple of culture-type birds sat on the battlements, or whatever you call them. One was named "Apathy" and the other "Prejudice." There was a telephone pole outside the castle, but the wires had been cut so they weren't leading anywhere.

I told Quig that I thought it was great—and I really did— but the only thing I didn't get the significance of, was the big insects labeled "WASPS" that were flying around.

"White, Anglo-Saxon, Protestant," Quig said. "*Wasp*. Isn't that the object of this school? To turn out people who are all right, all white, and up tight?" Quig really sounded sour. "No wonder the kids turn off or stare out windows or try to escape."

I just stared. I felt like you do when you take a lid off a kettle but instead of the gentle simmer you expect, you find that darned thing is boiling and ready to explode.

"I had another idea, too," Quig said, "but I decided on this."

"What was the other one?"

40

"I thought I might draw the school to look like a factory. It would show kids of all different shapes and sizes—you know, *individuals*—coming in one door of the school as freshmen, and then coming out a door on the other side as seniors. This time they would all look as alike as if they had been run through a stamping machine." Quig was looking at me as if he hoped I'd say I liked the second idea better. But I was too busy revising my opinion of Quig, who I'd always thought of as this quiet, perfectly square establishment-type, to say anything.

Quig went on. "I *like* the idea, but it would be better as a cartoon for the school paper. Though, of course, they wouldn't use it."

"No," I said. "They wouldn't." As a matter of fact, I was wondering if he'd get by showing the school as a crumbling castle with a lot of wasps flying around.

Quig wrapped the drawing up in the brown paper. "In any case, this one is going to make kids think."

"I don't know whether it's going to make them think," I said, "but it's going to make a lot of the Social-types sore."

Quig looked pleased. "That's why I wanted you to see it. To get a sort of man-in-the-street opinion."

"Yeah," I said. "That's me. But now, man, I've got to get going." Which I did. Although I had a good deal more sympathy with Quig wanting to make over Horace Greeley High than I did with Norm's plan to overthrow the capitalistic system, I'd had enough for a while. What I really needed was one of Mose Rubin's pastrami sandwiches on rye bread.

As it turned out, I didn't get my sandwich. Somebody'd thrown a rock through the window of the deli about two

41

minutes before I got there. Rubin was running back and forth on the sidewalk tearing his hair and yelling, "Police!"

I would have liked to stick around and watch the excitement, but when I saw a squad car coming with "Shad" at the wheel, I decided to make myself scarce. I didn't want any cops asking me questions about who did it. How did *I* know? Sure, I'd seen Curley Matthews hanging around the place at noon, but that didn't prove anything. And if there *was* a vendetta between him and the little Jew, it was no affair of mine. For all I knew, he had it in for me, too; as a result of walking out on him and Sherlie Lou at the drive-in. And it was enough tough luck that instead of a pastrami on rye I had to settle for a hamburger at the nearest McDonalds.

★ ★ ★ ★ ★ ★

Chapter 4

☆ ☆ ☆ ☆ ☆ ☆

I DIDN'T GO near headquarters for a couple of days, and when I did the first person I saw when I walked in was Watt Tyler. Although I shouldn't have been too surprised to see him, if I'd known he was going to be there I would have stayed away.

And if he was surprised to see me, he didn't show it. He's really pretty cool. Just looked up from a conversation he was having with Red Beard, said, "Hi, Doug," and went right on talking.

There was an empty chair a couple of feet away from Emily's desk, so I mooched on back there and straddled it so I faced her. She still hadn't looked up, but I knew if I sat there long enough staring at her she would have to. I've had people do it to me and it works. Always.

She wasn't hard to stare at, I'll tell you that. Although her hair was still skinned back, she'd parted it in the middle and brought it back above her ears so they showed. Never in all my life had I ever paid any attention to a girl's ears.

43

I mean, I'd certainly never thought they were sexy, but Emily Marlow's ears were. You'll just have to believe me. There were little pink patches of color in her cheeks, but the shadows I'd seen under her eyes on Friday weren't there any more.

I guess maybe I was staring harder than I intended, for just then she looked up.

"If you're just going to be sitting there," she said, "you might as well be doing something."

"Like doing what, for instance?" I didn't want to be sucked into doing a job that nobody else wanted to do, particularly with Watt Tyler looking on, so I had to be careful.

"Like taking these cards and finding out what congressional district the signers of these 'support' cards live in. I've already made a list of those who sent a contribution along with their card, so all you have to do is find their city or town on the map, then see what congressional district it's in. Those are in red so they're easy to find. After you get them all separated into piles, I'll tell you what to do next."

As Emily spoke, she shoved a shoe box full of yellow three-by-five-inch cards toward me. On each was a space for the person's name, address, city, and county. If they hadn't sent in money with their card, there was a place to indicate that they'd send some later or else help in the campaign some other way.

Emily had given me about a hundred cards and in the next half hour I didn't get through more than a dozen of them. Although the towns were listed alphabetically, many of them were so small you could hardly find them on the map even after you found out where they were supposed to be. Like Emily had said, the various congressional dis-

44

tricts were outlined in red, but even so they weren't all that easy to find because there were a lot of other red lines on the map showing rivers and roads.

Two other kids were sitting at the counter a little distance away who were apparently doing the same thing I was. But even at a glance I could tell that they were a lot faster than I was. I saw, too, that Watt Tyler was still there and hoped I might, at least, be making a good impression on him. It was a cinch I wasn't making *any* kind of an impression on Emily. She just went on slitting envelopes and taking out more yellow cards and shoving them in my direction.

It really looked as if I was stuck for a while and as I went on working the job did begin to get easier and, in a way, more interesting. There were, for example, a lot of cards from Garland City—that's where the state university is and where Norm goes to school—and it didn't take me too long before I remembered it was in the fourth district so I didn't have to look it up any more.

At five o'clock, the two kids who'd been working alongside of me got up and left and a little later an older woman I'd seen there before said if she wasn't home in time to get dinner for her husband he was going to leave her. Although she laughed when she said it, I noticed that she did get out of there in nothing flat. Finally, there wasn't anybody there but Watt Tyler and Red Beard, who were still talking, and Emily and me. Having lasted that long I decided I'd stay to the end.

I'd noticed a phone in one of the offices, so pretty soon I went back there to call my mother and tell her I wouldn't be home for dinner. She gave me the same old third degree

45

she's been giving me since I was old enough to be out alone. Where was I? What was I doing? Who was I with? And so on. The FBI missed a good investigator in my mother. But if she was good at the questions, I was good at the answers and I wound up the interview by saying that I was helping a friend of mine—true—and that I'd be sure to get something to eat. Also true. I do have this habit of eating three times a day.

When I came back from the phone and found that Watt Tyler and Red Beard had left at last, I guess maybe the shock was too much. I don't know. But instead of trying one more time to get Emily to go out with me, I reached for another pile of cards! Actually, some of the cards almost got me. For example, a character named Nathan Somebody who lived in a town called "Prairie," for God's sake, must have been at least ninety. His handwriting was so wiggly it looked as if it had been made by one of those machines that registers earthquakes, or something. In the space where it said "contributions" he'd written "fifty cents—wish I could do more." And a couple of cards later, there was one signed "Jim Dibbuk—aged 11." This kid said that as soon as he was twelve he could carry a paper route and that then he'd give a dollar! Kieran must have *something*, I thought, but I didn't think it would be the kind of something I liked. Norm said all politicians were phoney, and while I don't agree with very much of what Norm says, this time I was inclined to think he was right. Frankly, I thought that Kieran ought to be ashamed of himself, taking money from old men and little kids. But nobody had asked my opinion and I wasn't about to volunteer it, particularly as just then Emily pushed back her chair and announced in a voice as firm as if I had been arguing with her, that she was starved.

46

For a second, I felt as if I'd been pulling on a rope and then suddenly the guy at the other end let go, but I recovered fast. "OK," I said. "What are we waiting for? Come on, let's go."

Emily laughed. "We're not going anywhere. I've got a lot to do yet tonight. We'll eat right here." She reached in the bottom drawer of her desk for her purse, took out a dollar bill and a handful of change and pushed it toward me. "You can get pretty good hamburgers at Pete's Place, just around the corner. Two for you and one for me, and a couple of orders of french fries. I'll make some fresh coffee while you're gone. That in the pot tastes as if it had been made with lye water."

I stood up, leaving the money on the desk.

"Take it," Emily said. "I'm paying off a bet."

"Not with me."

"I know. I sort of lost a bet to myself . . . that you didn't come down here today to work, but to . . ."

"Goof around?"

"Something like that. But you fooled me." When she smiled, there was this kind of dimple that came in one cheek just above the corner of her mouth.

Although Pete's Place was pretty busy at that hour of the evening, in about fifteen minutes I was back at headquarters with the food. In addition to the hamburgers and french fries I'd gotten a couple of chocolate milk shakes. Emily had cleared off a place on the desk and made new coffee. Together we spread out the stuff.

It was a funny kind of date, sitting there in the middle of all that mess, but it was all right. I've spent a lot more money than that just to make out with a girl that I wasn't even too crazy about. And although I had about zero hopes

47

of making out with Emily until I could get her out of head-quarters and into The Bomb, it didn't matter that all we did was talk. Until I met her, I didn't know talk could be all that interesting. Part of it was because she was interesting. And maybe part of it was that she was interested in me. She asked a lot of questions about school, my folks, and what I liked best to do. I can't remember now exactly what I told her, but I leveled with her as much as I could without giving myself away.

What I liked best, though, was hearing about *her*. Although she was only a couple of months older than I was, she'd skipped a couple of grades somewhere along the line and was in her second year of college when Senator Kieran won the Presidential primary in New Hampshire. Pretty soon after that, he came to her campus to talk and just like that she decided that it was more important to help him get the nomination for President than it was to finish out the semester.

"I can't explain it too well, but the night he talked . . ." She put down what was left of her hamburger and kind of looked off in space as if she was trying to reconstruct just what happened. "The night he talked, he seemed to be talk-ing just to me. And he was saying all the things that I be-lieve in . . . that all wars are basically bad and that they never solve anything. That a way has to be found so there won't be any more. That it's not only wrong, in a country as rich as ours, for people to be going hungry but that a way has *got* to be found, right now, to remedy the situation. After the speech nearly all the other kids said they felt the same way. That he was talking to *them*. And that he believed, with their help, he could do something about it."

48

She was so sincere that her voice even shook a little as she talked. And I think she might even have convinced me that Kieran was the greatest guy who ever lived if, in my mind's eye, I couldn't see Norm sneering. And I knew what he'd say. That all this talk about making over the world, was just a lot of baloney, only that's not the word that Norm would have used. I'm not kidding, in an argument Norm would have demolished her, and I was glad he wasn't there.

In any case, she'd convinced her parents that leaving school to work for Kieran was the thing to do. And on top of that, they'd not only let her come halfway across the country to Cedar City to help organize the primary in our state, but were giving her money to live on while she did it.

From what she said, I don't think that they were all that rich, either. Her father was a social worker, her mother taught school, and there were a couple of younger brothers and sisters still at home.

Once while she was talking, she took off her glasses and laid them on the table but when she saw me staring at her she put them back on again and gave me a lecture on how necessary it was that everybody working for Kieran keep his mind on the campaign. "That doesn't mean we can't have fun. We can, and we do. But we're not *here* for fun, but to get Kieran nominated. That's the one thing Gabby insists on. That we all attend to business. And because we're serious, the word gets around. Even so, I don't know where everybody comes from. They just come flocking in, I guess, because they want to be involved and until Kieran came along there hasn't been anything for them to be involved in. Like you . . . for instance."

"Yeah." I felt the back of my neck start to prickle.

"Don't you see, that's why you've felt the way you do about school . . . about everything."

Emily paused, and just like that, I blew it. I said I had to be going.

For a second Emily looked startled then began stuffing the hamburger wrappings and french fries sack in the brown paper bag they'd come in. She was smiling again. "Sometimes I forget that just because I'm not in school, other people have homework to do. But anytime you can come down and help, do." She gave me that small-boy handshake. "And thanks for dinner, too."

I mumbled something and got out. I didn't know, myself, what had happened. For a while, it had been all right listening to her give this or that as the reason why I felt as I did about school, the draft, everything. Then suddenly, it wasn't all right any more.

I guess, maybe, I wanted her to like the *real* Doug Radigan —to like me as I was, though that wasn't very much—and not some phoney version of me she'd dreamed up. Like she had with Gregory Kieran.

I told myself that Emily had a hang-up and there wasn't any future for me hanging around headquarters. So I didn't. Actually, I think I might even have thought about her more than I did, if school hadn't happened to be a little less boring than usual. For American Government, Watt Tyler had assigned a couple of chapters in *Black Rage* and then let the kids start a discussion on it. Although I hadn't read it, most of the kids had and once or twice a couple of pretty good arguments developed. For the next class, Tyler had assigned a couple more chapters and this time I borrowed a copy of the book from a guy and did the reading. Even so, I don't think I'd have volunteered any opinions if Tyler hadn't called on me. I can't remember now what I said, but I guess it must have been all right because Tyler said I'd made a good point. Me. I had to laugh.

In English, all three days we had a substitute teacher, Miss Philbrick, and that helped. Anybody was better than Miss Beckman who always started off class with "A Thought for Today."

Friday morning when I went to school, Quig was waiting at my locker. He'd started talking before I had my coat off. "I thought you might like to know. I'm in trouble."

It stopped me. The idea of Quig being in trouble—any kind of trouble—was just about impossible to imagine.

"You'd better tell me," I said, even though it was almost time for the bell to ring. Quig really looked upset.

"About the drawing I made for the yearbook. You know, the one I showed you."

When I laughed, Quig just shook his head. "Maybe it doesn't sound like much, but I'm in trouble all the same. Yesterday, after school, I took my drawing in for Mr. Burch to look at. If you don't know, he's the faculty advisor for the yearbook and the Student Council, too."

I said I didn't know that, but I did know Burch, that I'd had him the year before for Home Room, and that he was so up tight about everything that he couldn't go to the john without calling a committee meeting.

Quig smiled at that, but said I'd missed the point. "*He* doesn't have to like the cover. The yearbook is a student publication and it ought to be up to the students, or a student committee of the Council, to judge it."

51

"Burch won't allow that?"

Quig gave a kind of hollow laugh. "I thought you said you knew him."

"Then why don't you take it to the Student Council? Isn't that what it's for? I mean, what's the use of being on it if you can't make a point now and then. There ought to be a bunch of kids who think the way you do."

"Are you kidding? Burch has them all in his pocket."

"How can you know that? For sure, I mean."

"Because right after I saw Burch, the Council met. As soon as I could get the floor, I showed them the drawing, explained what happened, then moved that Burch be rebuked. And no one said a word."

"You did *what?*"

"Moved that Burch be rebuked," Quig repeated. "It's a perfectly proper parliamentary procedure."

"What good does that do you," I said, "if it gets Burch down on you? You ought to have more sense." I was really about half sore. Not only had the bell rung while we were standing there, but Quig was looking as if I'd stabbed him between the second and third rib.

"Sorry," he said stiffly. "It's a matter of principle. Somehow, I thought you'd understand." With that he walked off leaving me with no choice but to go to see Steinfeld about getting back into class.

★ ★ ★ ★ ★ ★ ★

Chapter 5

☆ ☆ ☆ ☆ ☆ ☆ ☆

WHEN I GOT home, I looked up "rebuke" in the dictionary. It's a big one, like they have in the library at school. The folks had given it to Norm and me a couple of years before for Christmas, hoping that we'd make a lot of use of it. Norm did some, at first, but I almost never. That day, however, I was glad we had it.

Although there were a lot of definitions, they all added up to the same thing. Rebuke meant "to criticize severely." And there wasn't a thing that referred to parliamentary procedure. I wondered if Quig, maybe, hadn't just flipped. It just didn't make any sense—a kid who was going to have to get a scholarship if he was going to college, to boot everything because of some stupid drawing.

When I came down from the room over the garage that Dad calls the study, it was getting dark. I turned on the porch light for Mom and brought in the evening paper. Ever since I'd met Emily I'd been looking through it to see if there was anything about Senator Kieran. Watt Tyler was always after us, too, to read the newspaper so that worked out all right. Before I could look for any stories about Senator Kieran, though, a picture about four columns wide headed with a lot of big black type stopped me.

STATE STUDENTS ROUTED
IN SCIENCE HALL TAKEOVER

And there, being hauled away by two cops, was Norm. He was wearing the same outfit he'd had on when he was home the weekend before. The fringed suede jacket, tight jeans, and sandals, plus an Indian-type headband around his forehead.

The story went on to say that this was the latest in a series of confrontations between campus police and militant students demanding all-black dormitories. After they had successfully held the building for six hours, police said that anyone coming out peacefully would be released at once. Everybody came out but Norm. Naturally.

There was a lot more, including background material on a previous campus disorder which had been motivated by a demand for *integrated* dormitories, since agreed to. The president of the university announced that a new, hard line was going to be taken on any action that interfered with other students' free access to classes.

Standing there in the hall reading, I forgot all about Gregory Kieran. Instead, I was wondering if I could keep the paper from Mom. If I said the kid who lives down the street hadn't delivered it, she'd just call him and ask him to bring another one. But even if she didn't see the paper, she'd hear about Norm the next day at work. Some people are really glad when something bad happens to someone they

54

know, although they put on a big act about being sorry. I could just hear someone saying in this hushed voice, Norma, dear, I read in the paper last night about Norman. Though I know it isn't any fault of yours, *dear,* I do think it's terrible, don't you?

I didn't know whether it was terrible or not, the reason being that I didn't want to think about it.

I was still standing there when my mother opened the front door. "Oh, Dougie, you're home."

"Yeah, I'm home." Instinctively, like I'd done as a kid when I got caught with one hand in the cookie jar, I put the paper behind my back.

If my mother noticed, she didn't let on. A little later, when she went out to the kitchen to start dinner, I hid the paper behind the sofa.

Even when just the two of us were there alone, Mom always fixed things so they looked nice and all the while we were eating she kept up this kind of chatter about things that had happened at work that day. Not until after I'd finished my second piece of cake did she say, "What was there in the paper, Douglas, that you didn't want me to see?"

I shot her a quick look to gauge my chances for getting away with some kind of a lie and saw they weren't good.

"I want the truth, please, Doug. Is it about Norm?"

"Something about him."

I gave the paper to her and not knowing whether I ought to go or stay compromised, stood half in and half out of the kitchen. She read the story through without saying anything and all the time tears were welling up in her eyes until they spilled over. Then she shook her head as if that would make the whole thing go away, and then started clearing off the table with a lot of noise and scraping and running water in the sink.

I think, at that moment, if Norm had been there, I'd have knocked him down. Instead, I mumbled something about being sorry and went to the garage to do some work on The Bomb. I don't suppose I'd been there fifteen minutes before my mother called down to say a girl wanted to talk to me on the phone.

When I got to the top of the stairs I could see that my mother's eyes were still kind of red, but otherwise she was all right. "Monica?"

"Not Monica, but she sounds nice."

The caller turned out to be Emily. "Was that your mother who answered the phone? She sounds nice."

"She said the same about you."

"How's everything at headquarters?" I said, arranging myself for a nice long talk.

"Good, except for one thing. That's why I called."

With visions of more janitor service in mind, I sort of cooled off. "What seems to be wrong?" I asked.

"We're in this kind of a spot," said Emily. "Senator Kieran is talking in Maple City tomorrow night—it's his first major address in the state—and, of course, everybody wants to go. I thought I had enough cars lined up to take people who don't have any way to get there, but I'm still going to need another driver. I hoped maybe you . . ."

"*You're* going?"

Emily laughed. "Wild horses couldn't keep me away. Or is it only wild horses who try to drag people *away* from somewhere? But you mustn't worry about me. I'll find a niche somewhere."

56

I wasn't worried about her finding a niche, I was just afraid it might not be with me.

"It's perfectly all right if you can't go," Emily said apologetically. "I do understand. But I thought it was worth calling you to find out. Fortunately, there was just one Radigan in the phone book."

"Hey," I said. "Wait. I'm thinking. Maybe I could make it. What time is Kieran speaking?"

"Eight o'clock in the evening. At the college. Maple City is about a two-hour drive on the interstate. But to be on the safe side, we ought to leave by four thirty or so." She didn't add, "Douglas, please," but I heard it loud and clear all the same.

"I can make it," I said. "For you."

"For Senator Kieran."

"For you."

"Have it your own way." She laughed again. "Good night."

"Hey," I said. "Wait!" But it didn't do any good. She had gone.

All the while I'd been talking on the phone, I could see my mother bobbing around in the other room. I knew she was dying to know who I'd been talking to, so I told her that a girl I knew wanted me to drive some kids to Maple City to hear Gregory Kieran talk at a political rally.

"Isn't he the one your father doesn't like?"

I said that as far as I knew my father didn't like any of the candidates.

"Maybe it would be better," my mother said, pretending not to hear, "if you could avoid telling your father where you were going." She spoke as if it settled everything.

57

"If he asks me, I'll tell him," I said, not thinking it necessary to say that as far as I was concerned, Gregory Kieran could jump in the middle of Cedar Lake and never come up.

An hour or so later after I'd come upstairs, the phone rang again. My mother answered it, and this time it was my father.

You don't have to be a mind reader to know certain things. Even without listening, I knew that my father wherever he was, had either bought a newspaper where he'd read about Norm or else he'd heard it on the ten-o'clock news.

I closed my door. I didn't want to hear my mother's side of the conversation but the walls of the houses in Paradise Acres are thin and make for togetherness whether you want it or not.

When my mother said, "But Norm is as much your son as he is mine," I knew that my father had delivered his famous line, "Look what your son has done now."

I went down the hall to the bathroom and turned on the shower full force so I wouldn't have to hear any more.

I don't know what time my father got home that night but the next day around noon when I went out to the kitchen to get something to eat he was there talking to my mother. They must have been discussing Norm, for they stopped when they saw me. My father gave me a sort of vacant look, asked me how I was, then went down to his workshop. A moment later I heard his power saw buzzing away. I only hoped he wouldn't cut off a thumb or finger.

After lunch I went down to Quig's station to buy gas and get the oil checked before going down to headquarters. "You can be glad you weren't here five minutes ago," Quig said, giving me a funny look. "Curley was in looking for you. With a knife."

58

Although I laughed, for Quig's benefit, I was remembering what Curley had said he was going to do to me.

It was about three thirty when I got to headquarters. Red Beard was there, also Joe and Molly, the stringy-haired girl, and a couple of other people I'd never seen before. These included a tall thin black boy, a girl who looked as if she was going to have a baby any minute, a stocky, gray-haired woman, and a fat kid wearing glasses.

My pal Emily was nowhere in sight. If there hadn't been about one chance in a thousand that she was in one of the back offices, I'd have left right then. I knew without anyone telling me who was going to ride in The Bomb with me to Maple City. The black boy, the fat kid, the stocky old lady, and the girl who was going to have a baby.

Before I was more than two feet inside the door, however, Red Beard leaped up to greet me. "Emily told me to tell you she had to leave early this morning for Maple City. As you can imagine, there are a lot of loose ends to take care of. But she did want you to know that she appreciated your offer to drive." He began rustling papers around on his desk. "Now, let's see. Gribbles doesn't have a ride. And Dodie doesn't nor Mike Bridges. You know Grib, Dodie, and Mike?"

I said I didn't, but I could guess. And I was right, of course. A second later Red Beard was introducing me to Tom Gribbles, the tall black kid, Dodie Pembroke, the girl who was going to have a baby, and Mike Bridges, the fat boy.

"Pete D'Mario left word yesterday that he needs a ride, too," Red Beard went on. "He's not here yet, but he ought to be along pretty soon. In the meantime, this is the plan. Go to the airport, first—if you have time. Kieran's plane arrives from Chicago at six forty. Join the caravan of cars that will

59

follow him to the college where he's going to talk. If there's not time for that—and remember, you'll have a heck of a time finding a place to park at the airport—go directly to the college. There's a section reserved for Cedar City in the auditorium. Of course, there may be such a mob you won't be able to sit with our gang. But if that happens, well, that's its own compensation." He grinned. "Any questions?"

The only question I had was how I'd ever let myself get mickey-moused into spending part of Saturday afternoon and all that evening driving four hundred miles to hear a speech by somebody I couldn't vote for even if I wanted to.

"While you're waiting for Pete to show, you can fold these letters I'm signing and put them in these addressed envelopes."

By four o'clock the kid named D'Mario hadn't shown so Red Beard gave me—you guessed it—Mrs. Peacham, the stocky, gray-haired lady. Red Beard, himself, left about the same time with a cute girl who came to pick him up in a red Karmann Ghia.

With my assortment of passangers, I couldn't care less who sat with me in the front seat as long as it wasn't Dodie. Fortunately, she arranged herself in the back seat with Mrs. Peacham and Mike Bridges, the fat boy. Gribbles got up in front with me.

Right away Mrs. Peacham and Dodie started talking as if they'd known each other for years, and maybe they had. I didn't listen—there isn't anything that interests me less than babies—and concentrated on getting out of town and on the interstate as soon as possible.

This Gribbles didn't say a word, just sat there. Though he wasn't the Panther type—he didn't have an Afro haircut and he wasn't wearing chains or beads like some of Norm's black

60

friends did—still, you never can tell, and the thought passed briefly through my mind that maybe he was a Panther in disguise.

Though I'd pushed the front seat as far back as it would go to give me leg room, Gribbles' legs were so long they were jackknifed in front of him. His hands, one of which lay face up in his lap, could have held a basketball as easy as a girl's hand would hold a tennis ball.

"You play basketball?"

"A couple of years ago, I played guard for Central High."

I said, "Oh," feeling foolish. Even though I don't follow basketball the way I do football and baseball, I should have recognized Gribbles. Central had won the state basketball tournament that year and Gribbles' picture had been plastered all over the sport pages most of one winter.

"You're not playing now? I mean, why aren't you playing in college? I'd have though you'd get some pretty good offers."

Gribbles grinned. "I got the offers. This just isn't my time to go."

I had to let it drop at that, though I would have liked to know the reason. Gribbles himself was quiet, too, which I sort of appreciated. When I'm driving, I'm not one for doing a lot of talking. Besides, there was enough conversation in the back seat to make up for any lack of it in front. All three were telling how they happened to be working for Senator Kieran. Then Mrs. Peacham, who must have been a teacher, started explaining how Presidential primaries first got started. Which you would think would be straight from Dullsville. But before I could tune her out, I got sort of interested.

In fact, if I'd thought about it at all, I would have supposed

61

that all states had Presidential primaries like we do, and had always had them. But that was wrong. About 1903, in Wisconsin, a bunch of people, headed by a guy named Robert La Follette, who called themselves Progressives took over the Republican party and decided that it wasn't right for politicians to get together at the convention and choose the man they wanted to run for President; that the people ought to have something to say about it, too. Soon after, Wisconsin held the first state-wide primary. And by 1910, seven more states decided to do the same thing.

There were a lot of other reforms the Progressives were after and finally got—like child labor laws and the workmen's compensation acts. Another, was that senators get elected by the people the same way representatives did, instead of being selected by the state legislatures. They helped get an amendment to the Constitution that gave women the right to vote and got rid of a lot of crookedness that railroad, telephone, and electrical companies were up to.

Though Senator Kieran didn't call himself a Progressive, she said he had the same kind of goals and that a lot of new reforms were needed today. To hear her talk, you'd have thought this guy walked about two inches off the ground. But nobody was asking my opinion and I didn't volunteer it.

When we were about two-thirds of the way to Maple City, this same old bird trotted out some ham salad sandwiches on homemade bread, potato chips, and brownies for everybody and by the time we'd finished the lot we were almost there.

Dodie then said she thought we ought to poll the delegation to see whether we ought to go to the airport to meet Kieran when he arrived or go straight to the college.

Everybody but me, and I didn't vote, was for going

straight to the auditorium in order to be sure we got a chance to sit in our own section.

I guess it's a good thing we decided that way, though at the time it didn't make any difference to me. There turned out to be a pretty big parking place, but it was already filled and we had to leave The Bomb a couple of blocks away in somebody's yard. The owner had lettered a big sign PARK-ING, $1.00, and was standing out in front of his house with a flashlight trying to get people to come in and park.

"Grandma" said she'd pay the buck and by a quarter of seven we were on our way back to the college auditorium. I was still walking with Gribbles, and Mike, Dodie, and "Grandma" were walking behind. But if anybody thought we were a funny-looking crew, nobody said anything.

It wasn't too cold, but just cold enough so you weren't uncomfortable. The crowds on the sidewalk were getting thicker by the minute, and by the time we were in the quarter block that led to the auditorium we were almost shoulder to shoulder with people of every age, shape, and description. Nobody shoved or even seemed impatient. I can't exactly explain it. People were just in a good mood, that's all. A few people, kids of college age mostly, were carrying banners and hand-lettered signs that said "Kieran Cares" and a cop on a motorcycle rode slowly along next to the sidewalk to keep the crowds out of the street.

Inside the auditorium, however, it was really wild. There were about a dozen different aisles in the place and a couple of guys stood at the entrance telling people where to go. No matter where you looked there was somebody with a ribbon on his chest saying OFFICIAL scurrying around and here and there tables had been set up where girls were selling

63

"Kieran Cares" buttons, bumper stickers, and stuff like that.

It was past seven o'clock by my watch when the five of us got inside and were directed to a section of the auditorium about halfway down on the right-hand side. And there, believe it or not, was Emily. With her was Watt Tyler, a girl he introduced as his wife, and a couple of other people I'd seen around headquarters whose names I didn't know. In the next fifteen minutes or so a dozen more people sat down in our section so I assumed that they were from Cedar City, too.

All the time a band way down in front kept playing rah-rah music. One piece in particular must have been a special Kieran song because they kept playing it over and over again, faster and faster, until everybody in the place was singing and keeping time. I didn't want to, but it was easier to do it than not. Emily had skinned her hair back, but not as tightly as usual, and she was wearing a dress. I'd never seen her before in anything but pants and I hoped she'd never wear them again.

Looking back on it now, the whole thing is kind of hard to explain. Maybe part of it was mob psychology, though Emily explained to me later that that wasn't Kieran's appeal at all, but the minute Kieran appeared you could feel this kind of electrical impulse.

He came walking quite fast down the center aisle—one guy was ahead of him, another behind, and one on either side—and up on the platform. In the meantime, everybody had stood up and was whistling and clapping. I did it, too. You couldn't help yourself. But I disapproved of it. I mean, I didn't like the idea of a lot of people getting themselves all worked up over a politician. Then he started to talk. Not reading, or even looking at the speech he held in his hand, but talking as quietly as if he was sitting across the table from you in your own house.

Later, a lot of copies of that talk were printed and we had a pile of them at headquarters to give to people who wanted them. I wish now I'd taken one, because to tell you the truth I wasn't paying all that much attention to what he said.

I remember, though, that people laughed when he said that when there was something politicians either didn't understand, or didn't want understood, that usually they gave it a Latin word. Though I don't suppose too many of the kids there ever had studied Latin—I know I hadn't—but they got the idea when he said that's where the word "escalation" came from. And that all the new words out of the Pentagon like "pacification," "rectification," and "ratios" came about the same way.

This was kind of a jumping-off point for talking against "militarization," if that's the word, as a way of solving anything. Like half the nations of the world having American military missions, and us giving military aid to practically every country who asks us for it. With the result that our military gets involved with *their* military and a situation develops that we can't get out of. Like Viet Nam. And all the time we are selling guns and planes and ammunition to other countries. Sometimes we say we do it in the name of defense, sometimes diplomacy and sometimes just to get rid of our own military mistakes.

All this while, Emily's eyes were shining like Christmas tree lights, but when he took a crack at the Government giving about a half billion bucks to colleges and universities for military research, without being very particular as to what the grants or researches were for, then advocated giving eighteen-year-olds the vote, because he said it was *their* future, that did it. She reached over and squeezed my hand. "Isn't he *wonderful!*" she breathed. "Isn't he *marvelous?*"

It took me less than a second to say "yes." If he was good enough for a smart girl like Emily Marlow, he had to be good enough for me. Besides, what I'd heard of Kieran's talk did make a kind of sense.

Chapter 6

☆ ☆ ☆ ☆ ☆ ☆ ☆

THERE WAS PLENTY in the Sunday paper the next day about Senator Kieran's Maple City speech. It had the big headline on page one, and a long story that jumped over to an inside page. There was an interview with Kieran at the airport, a full page of pictures, and something called a "news analysis," in which the writer tried to figure out what this thing was that Kieran had that was turning people on, kids particularly.

I read every word. In fact, it was kind of exciting just to know that I'd been there. I just wished I had somebody to talk to about it.

Later that day, I drove down to headquarters hoping I might find someone there. The place, however, was closed up tight and I was just leaving when I remembered the key that was always supposed to be left at the filling station across the street.

The kid who was working there gave it to me and a few minutes later I was inside. With no typewriters going, machines running, phones ringing, or kids talking, it was quiet enough in there to give you the creeps. Still, I was kind of glad to have a chance to look around on my own. I'd never worn a Kieran button, but when I found a bowlful of them on a table near the door, I put one on. There were some windshield stickers, too, and as I put a couple of these in my pocket, leaving some change in another bowl on the table to pay for them, I heard a rattle at the door.

It was Emily.

She said, "Douglas!" in a pleased way, stamping the snow off her boots and unwinding a scarf about twelve feet long from around her neck and head.

She wasn't wearing her glasses and her cheeks were red from the cold, like a little kid's. "As soon as I pick up some signature cards, I'm going out to Watt Tyler's. I don't know who'll be there, but I'm sure it would be all right if you came along."

"Ever-ready Radigan," I said, though I wasn't sure that Mr. Tyler would be as crazy to see me as all that.

I carried the box of cards out to The Bomb, and while Emily locked up, I took the key to the filling station across the street.

It was still snowing, and big fat soft flakes caught in Emily's eyelashes as we walked toward the car. Once inside, I turned on the heater and found some nice music on the radio. Which would have made things practically perfect if I'd been starting out on a date, instead of going to a teacher's house to discuss politics.

But that's the way it was, and after Emily had told me where Watt Tyler lived, the best I could do was drive slowly and take the longest route possible to get there.

The street he lived on wasn't much. Just ordinary houses,

68

some two-stories with a little porch out in front, others not much bigger than a cracker box. All were set on small lots. Somehow, I guessed Watt Tyler would have lived in a better neighborhood. Yet when I remembered how young he was, it was kind of surprising that he had a house at all.

Emily pointed out a two-story house, tannish below and brown shingles up above as his. There was a VW bus in the drive, and two cars and a motorbike parked out in front. The sidewalk had been shoveled once, but fresh snow had since fallen and we squeaked our way through it up on the porch. Besides, a rug to wipe your feet on there was a baby buggy. Either Watt Tyler was a father, which surprised me, or else he was recruiting younger workers than I thought.

Watt Tyler came to the door. "Hi, Emily. Hi, Doug. Come on in. The faithful are gathering. You can just throw your wraps on the bench there in the hall."

There were about a dozen people already there, all of them kids. A few I'd seen around Kieran headquarters before. Several went to Greeley High. The rest were new to me.

The chairs were all taken, so Emily and I sat on the floor. Everybody said "hello" and Watt Tyler went on with what he'd been talking about when we came in. How to get people to sign support cards for Kieran.

"Almost everything in a political campaign costs money. But knocking on doors—that's free. There really isn't a 'right' way to go about it. Any way is right if the person agrees to go to the polls on the twenty-first and vote for Senator Kieran. But I might give you an example." He looked around the room. "Emily, do you want to be the lady of the house?"

69

"I may not be in too good a mood," Emily said, making like a tired housewife. "I'm in the basement washing."

Watt Tyler grinned. "Then I'd better knock again." He cracked his knuckles on the arm of his chair.

"OK. I'm coming upstairs. Now I'm opening the front door," Emily said. "Yes?" She made the final word sound sharp and upleasant.

"Good morning. I'm John Jones," Watt Tyler said. "I'm working for Senator Gregory Kieran. I would appreciate . . ."

Emily cut him off. "We're for Governor Frazier here," Emily said. "Slam!"

"Wow!" Watt Tyler ducked and grinned. "OK. Next lady. Knock, knock."

"Yes?"

"I'm John Jones. I'm working for Senator Gregory Kieran and I would appreciate your voting for him in the primary Tuesday, February twenty-first."

"I don't know much about him." Emily sounded doubtful.

"I have some literature to leave with you. You might like to look it over. This sheet gives you a brief biography and this is his voting record in the Senate. And this sheet outlines the issues and where the Senator stands on them."

"Thank you." Still sounding like the lady, Emily took the imaginary sheets. "I'll read it, and I'll have my husband read it, too."

"Thank you, good-bye, end of interview," Watt Tyler said. "Now let's talk to a third lady. Ready, Emily?"

Emily said, "Ready," and once again Watt Tyler made his little speech about working for Senator Kieran, and this time Emily said she was "interested."

70

"Perhaps, then, you'd like to sign this support card." Watt Tyler whisked out one of the yellow cards. "If you can make a contribution to the campaign, it would be appreciated. But if you can't give money, perhaps you could work for the Senator."

Emily said she couldn't give any money but would be glad to work, and Watt Tyler said, "Cut!" then once more was himself. "That, kids, is roughly the way it will go. But no matter what kind of a reaction you get, don't lose your cool. Be sincere, be polite, be yourselves. Remember you are affecting the political system in the best and most basic way—by getting people to vote. If there aren't any questions, I'll give you envelopes with your material in it and the areas you are to cover. And don't forget, we need more workers. Anyone you find who's willing to canvas, send him to me."

All the while Watt Tyler had been talking, I had the uneasy feeling that I wasn't going to get out of the house without taking one of the brown envelopes with me. Wearing a Kieran button was one thing, but taking my valuable time to work for the guy was something else again.

Emily, who'd disappeared, returned a few minutes later. "I got you *two* envelopes," she said. "It's really kind of fun, knocking doors, once you get the hang of it." She then went away again and this time when she came back she said we could go.

This raised my spirits, but on our way to the car she dashed them again. She said she had to go home.

"Home!" I yelped. "It's too early! Besides, I want to get something to eat! Go for a little ride! Something, Emily . . . please?"

Emily shook her head. "I'm sorry, Doug. I explained be-

71

fore how it is. And I really do have things to do. I'll tell you where I live."

It turned out to be a big old house that had been converted into a kind of home for working girls. Emily admitted it was pretty dismal, but that it had the advantage of only being a few blocks from headquarters.

The Bomb's wheels had hardly stopped rolling before Emily started to get out.

"Hey!" I said. "Don't be in such a big fat hurry. You can stay and talk for a few minutes, can't you?" I reached across her and shut the car door which she'd already got opened.

"Not really. It's getting dark, and . . ."

"I know," I said. "That's why it would be nice just to sit here quietly and, well, talk." She was wearing enormous mittens made out of some kind of shaggy fur. I pulled one off her hand and held it between both of my own. "Emily," I said, in this real, soft voice, "please." But she wasn't having any of that either. Pulling away, she reached again for the door and I knew she'd be out of there and up the sidewalk unless I thought of something fast. And, just like that, it came to me. The business about Quig. I was pretty sure she'd go for that.

"Hey!" I said. "There's something important I have to ask your advice about—something that happened at school."

When she took her hand off the door, and kind of halfway sat back in the seat, I gave it to her as fast as I could about Quig's father dying, about Quig having to work, and all of his younger brothers and sisters depending on him, and then winding up with the business of the drawing for the year-book being turned down, and Quig rebuking the faculty advisor.

"Quig sounds like quite a boy," Emily said. Her voice was a little husky and I was afraid that maybe I'd made too good a story out of Quig and his troubles.

"The way Quig tells it," I said, "what he did is perfectly all right. The rules you run meetings by, he says, allow you to. *I* don't know. But I thought maybe you would."

"I'm not terribly up on parliamentary procedures, but I'm pretty sure he's right about the 'rebuking' bit. I know that senators or congressmen can vote to censure a member if they think he's done wrong, and I'd think 'rebuke' adds up to about the same thing."

"Well, no matter about that," I said. "What worries me, is that Quig may just be throwing away the ball game to prove a point. He's got a lot more at stake than just getting that drawing on the cover of the yearbook. Like getting a free ride to college, for instance."

Emily shook her head. "Sorry, Doug. But I'm on Quig's side. One thing I've learned from Senator Kieran is that while compromise may be better than nothing, it still isn't right." She was terribly in earnest and hadn't noticed that I was holding her hand again. Or if she noticed she didn't pull it away. "One's own motives must never be suspect. I don't mean that yours are, because I know you want to help Quig. And you can."

"Yeah?" I guess maybe I sounded a little surprised. After all, I hadn't even known I wanted to help Quig until I heard her say so.

"Quig needs your support. He needs to know that somebody's behind him. In a democratic society, everyone has to do his part. And at every level. Even at school."

I moved in a little closer to Emily, and without her noticing got one arm up on the back of the seat behind her neck. "How?" I said. "How can I help?"

"By going before the Student Council. Ask that *they* vote on whether the drawing ought to be accepted or rejected. Or, better yet, ask that they put it to a vote of the entire student body, and not let it be decided by a faculty advisor." It was really getting dark now, and Emily's eyes were shining. "Please, Doug, say that you will."

"Sure, baby," I said softly. "If you want me to, I will." I was close enough to her now to brush my lips against her cheek, but only for about an instant. The next instant she was saying, "Good!" very briskly and with a quick scoot away from me had got the door opened and one foot outside.

"Hey!" I said. "Wait! I'm going with you. Don't they have a parlor or a sitting room, or something, where kids can . . ."

"They have one," Emily said. "But I don't use it."

"Then I'll go to the door with you."

"No, Doug, I'd rather you didn't. Good night." Like that, she ran up a steep flight of steps, turned to wave once, then opened the door and went inside.

As I sat there in The Bomb thinking about how crazy I was about Emily and also what a first-class boob I was—if she asked me to climb to the top of the KCCC-TV transmission tower and jump off, I'd probably do it—a car that had been parked across the street began to move, headlights off, toward the corner. As it passed beneath a street light I saw that it was Curley Matthews' psychedelic Dodge.

I waylaid Quig at his locker the next morning. Try as

hard as I could, I couldn't figure out any way of getting out of doing what Emily had asked me to do. "Hey," I said. "What's new with Burch and the Student Council?"

Quig looked gloomy. "All I know is that he's got somebody else drawing the cover and that I'm in the doghouse."

"I thought maybe you'd had another meeting," I said, "and this time you moved to impeach the guy."

Quig looked so down I decided not to fool around any longer. "I know somebody who's on your side."

"Who?"

"Me," I said. "I am."

"Oh," Quig said, looking disappointed. "Thanks a lot. But I don't know what you could do."

"There's one thing," I said. "I could speak to the Student Council in your behalf." I cleared my throat. "Ladies and Gentlemen. 'I come to bury Casesar, not to praise him. The evil that men do lives after them,' . . ."

Quig grinned. "That's the wrong speech. *I* haven't done any evil. But the idea's all right. The Council meets Friday, before school, if you want to come."

I held up my right hand in a gesture of peace. "Do not fear, Doug is here."

Quig made a fist and gave me a friendly poke in the chest. It made me feel good. He hadn't done that in a long time.

I don't know what Student Council meetings are like at your school. Maybe you run them differently. I hope so. Me, I'd never been to one before.

Ours met in the auditorium. I guess it was the only place big enough to hold it. Though until the day I turned up to speak for Quig, I'd never thought about how many home

75

rooms there were, and how many Student Council representatives there would have to be in a school of almost two thousand kids.

Quig and I had decided it would be better if we didn't sit together, so while Quig went down in front where all the representatives were gathered in a clump, I sat down over at one side and back a couple of rows.

The meeting hadn't started yet and kids kept going up and down the steps that led to the stage where Burch, the faculty advisor, and Monica—who, I guessed, was secretary—sat behind a study hall table. The president, a square-looking kid whose name was Rodney Van Pratt, was already standing behind a lecture stand in the middle of the stage rattling papers.

After Van Pratt said, "The weekly meeting of the Horace Greeley High student governing body will now come to order," three times, Burch clomped on the table with a ruler and things quieted down.

After that, I didn't listen much. Just enough so I would recognize my cue. And what I did hear, didn't sound very interesting. The "Porpoises," the girls' swimming club, was having a "Swim-In" with proceeds to go to the starving Snirfabi. Students found in violation of parking regulations on the school grounds would be fined. Motions were made, seconded, and passed with the smoothness of a well-oiled piece of machinery.

If I wasn't exactly calm while I waited, I wasn't nervous either. It doesn't bother me to talk, as you've probably guessed by now. Anyway, a couple of days before, Quig and I had written out what I was going to say and if I did forget all I had to do was look at the piece of paper in my hand.

76

"Any new business?" said Van Pratt.

That was my cue. I stood up. "Yes," I said. "My name is Douglas Radigan."

Seats squeaked, and necks craned as I spoke. It was the most exciting thing that had happened so far.

"I don't know you," Rodney Van Pratt said. "Are you a member of the Student Council?"

"No. But I'm a member of the student body." I would have liked to add "in good standing" just to make it sound better, but I wasn't sure I was.

Rodney Van Pratt looked at Burch, the faculty advisor, who shook his head and said something in a voice too low for me to hear.

"If you want to talk about that rejected cover for the yearbook, you are out of order," Van Pratt said.

"Something's out of order, but it's not me," I said.

Once more Van Pratt looked to Burch for advice, got the nod, and again thumped with his gavel. "I said, you were out of order, so sit down. Or better yet, get out. This isn't an open meeting of the Council. As I was saying, is there any new business?"

"Monkey business," I said. Even then, I wasn't too mad. Maybe because none of what was happening seemed real. It was more like one of the nutty dreams I sometimes have where I find myself doing some kind of nutty thing I'd never do if I was awake. "Now, if you'll just let me say what I came to say . . ."

Once more Van Pratt started pounding with his gavel. Somebody yelled, "Let him talk!" But it didn't do any good. Then just like that, something snapped inside my head. Like a robot I moved away from my seat and started down the aisle toward the stage. Quig leaped out to intercept me, I brushed him aside, and that was as far as I got. A guy had appeared on either side of me, each about seven feet tall and weighing two hundred and fifty pounds. Right guard and left guard on the unbeaten Greeley High football team. I let them turn me around and walk me up the aisle and out the big double doors into the hall. Both were embarrassed. One said, "Sorry, buddy." The other said, "That's what sergeants at arms are for."

Quig, who'd managed to get out of the auditorium ahead of us, waited until the "team" had left. He looked pale. "I shouldn't have let you try," he said. "I should have known that's what would happen."

I shook my head, hoping he would stop talking. Or just go away. I wasn't mad at him. I wasn't mad at anybody anymore, though I had been, inside. It was funny. I just had this kind of feeling—I can't explain it—that I'd lost something. I felt in my pants pocket for my car keys and billfold where I keep my driver's license. Without them, I'd really be out of luck. But that wasn't it. They both were there.

★ ★ ★ ★ ★ ★ ★

Chapter 7

☆ ☆ ☆ ☆ ☆ ☆ ☆

WHEN I GOT home from school, I was surprised to find my father already there. He still had on his good suit—usually he puts on work pants and an old shirt first thing—and he looked out of place. Another thing, he wasn't doing anything, which he most always is. When I came in he was just kind of milling around the living room picking up and looking at some of the doodads Mom has sitting around. She's crazy about these miniature statues, figurines she calls them, of kids and animals.

For a second, I had this feeling that he was waiting to talk to me. But that didn't make sense. I guess you can say that my dad and I hadn't really talked to each other in years. There'd been a time, though I couldn't remember exactly when, when he and Norm and I had done things together. And for a while, we'd talked a lot about the things we were going to do. Camping was one of them. We were going to get a tent that would sleep three and go camping. We weren't going to take a lot of supplies, just the essentials, and take the rest off the land. We'd fish, shoot rabbits, or better yet we'd trap them.

"I'm home early," my father said, just as if I couldn't see him.

"Yeah."

"Do you want to know why?" My father sounded edgy.

"Sure," I said. "Why?"

"Because I couldn't take the gaff any longer. Because since last Monday when I started out on the road, every place I went, every customer I saw, wanted to know if that kid named Radigan who was in trouble at the university was my son." He stopped, put down this little china dog he was holding, and then went on. "As soon as I said 'yes,' people seemed to be sorry they'd asked. They were sorry for me. So instead of finishing my territory, I came on home."

I said I didn't blame him for that but he went on as if he hadn't heard me. "And if Norm comes home this weekend, I'm leaving again. I don't want to see him. I don't want to talk to him. Your mother and I will just go somewhere. We'll drive over to Danville to see your Aunt Rita, and if your mother doesn't want to do that, we'll go to a motel."

"Maybe he won't come home," I said.

"Ha!" said my father, but he wasn't laughing. "That's what gets me. Coming home to sleep in a bed with clean sheets, stuff himself on your mother's cooking, and all the time spouting off about the dehumanizing process of the monopolistic oligarchies that run our society. So I'm giving you fair warning that I'm not going to be here. Call me when your mother gets home, I'm going to take a nap."

After he'd gone, I left to call Emily and tell her what had happened at the Student Council meeting. She wasn't at headquarters, though, and Red Beard, who answered the phone said she was out door-knocking and didn't know
80

when she'd be back. I was about ready to hang up when I remembered to ask if he happened to know *where* she was door-knocking. I knew they had this big map of the city and a master list of all the people who were registered voters in every precinct.

Red Beard said to wait a minute and he'd see if he could find out. I held on and pretty soon he was back again to say that he couldn't be very specific about it, but he thought she was canvassing the Chesterfield district and that she might very well have begun at Fourth and Fillmore.

I said that was good enough for me and it was. Even if I didn't find Emily, it would get me out of the house for a while. If Norm came home I didn't want to be there any more than my father did.

The Chesterfield district isn't a good one and personally I thought Red Beard was out of his head to let Emily go there to knock doors, particularly when it was beginning to get dark. On the other hand, I knew that if Emily had made up her mind she wanted to go there, she would.

Actually, I didn't have very much hope of finding her, so when I saw her after fifteen minutes or so of riding around, I was pretty surprised. She was just coming down the rickety steps of a big old house with a "Rooms for Rent" sign in the front window, and putting some papers and stuff back into the big brown envelope she was carrying.

I stopped The Bomb, rolled down the window and said, "Hey! Emily!" I didn't say it very loud, but she still jumped a little.

"Oh, Doug," she said. "It's you."

I said, "Get in. I want to talk to you."

"Can't. I've got a couple of more blocks still to do. I don't

81

know whether you realize we haven't covered even half the city yet and the primary is a little more than two weeks away. How are you coming with your territory?"

For a minute, I couldn't think what she was talking about. Then I remembered the two brown envelopes she'd pushed off on me the night we went to the meeting at Watt Tyler's house. When I'd come home that night I'd stuffed them into one of my bureau drawers. "Oh, fine," I said. "Just fine."

Emily stepped back from the car. "Well, I'd better get going."

"Hey," I said. "Wait a minute. Why don't you take one side of the street and I'll take the other? That way, we'll get through twice as fast."

"If you're sure you want to."

"Sure I'm sure," I said. "Give me some of your stuff."

Emily scrambled around in her envelope, gave me a stack of the yellow "support" cards and some literature. "I'll meet you at the corner of Sixth and Fillmore. There's a drugstore there. See you."

By the time I pulled The Bomb into the curb, Emily was already standing in the lighted doorway of the next house on her side of the street. I could see her talking, but she didn't go in and I was glad of that. I just hoped Emily wasn't watching me. If anyone answered my knock, which after a couple of minutes I was beginning to doubt, I'd probably get the door slammed in my face. But it didn't work out that way at all. Somebody finally came. A girl, no older than me, carrying a fat baby boy. And though the house looked crummy on the outside, inside it wasn't all that bad. A guy was sitting in front of a television set which was going full blast, watching the news, and I could smell dinner cooking.

82

It took me a minute before I could remember what I was supposed to say and when I did come out with my name and information that I was working for Senator Kieran, she turned to the guy watching television and said, "We're for Senator Kieran, aren't we, Les." He grinned and said, "You're damned right we are. I can't give you any money, but I'll sign that card you've got there."

I watched as he signed it, and in spite of what he said, he dug around in one of his pants pockets and handed me a dollar bill along with the card. "Maybe Kieran can't make over the world, but at least he can make a few improvements in the kind of world my kid is going to live in."

That kind of got to me, and before I went to the house next door I took a couple of deep breaths before knocking.

It was a good thing I did, because a woman with her hair in curlers slammed the door so hard when she saw me, it almost knocked me off my feet.

After that, it seemed mostly back and forth, though when I added up the score after I got to the drugstore where I was to meet Emily I discovered that of the twenty houses I'd gone to, seven signed support cards for Senator Kieran. Six others were for Governor Frazier, and four were for Swallow. The rest didn't plan to vote.

A couple of minutes later, Emily came bouncing in and when we compared notes I found she'd had pretty good luck, too.

"OK," I said. "Let's celebrate. We'll go to a drive-in and get something to eat and then maybe go to a movie."

"Oh, dear," said Emily. "I can't. I've got Gabby's car and I've got to get it back to him. It's parked just around the corner."

I was so frustrated that I put my head down on the soda-fountain counter upsetting a glass of water which ran down on my pants.

"Douglas!" said Emily, sounding alarmed. "Is something wrong? Don't you feel well?"

I sopped up the water on my pants and tried to get hold of myself. "I feel all right," I said. "I just wanted to talk to you." I was whining like a five-year-old who had his candy taken away from him, but I didn't care.

"We can talk right here for a while," Emily said soothingly. "We'll just order a couple of Cokes. Two Cokes, please," she said to the clerk who was sort of hovering around. "Large ones."

They appeared and she paid for them before I could get my money on the counter.

"Now tell me," Emily said. "Is it about school?"

I said it was, then told her everything that had happened, winding up with the really awful way I felt when I was put out of the Council meeting without a chance to make my speech. But even before I finished, Emily was quivering.

"Of course, you felt awful!" she cried. "You were denied one of your inalienable rights guaranteed by the Constitution."

"I was?"

"The right of free speech!" She was still intense. "Too often we do not realize what we have lost until it has been taken away from us. That is what Senator Kieran has been teaching us. That's what the 'new politics' is all about. The only lasting accomplishment in Government arises from the beliefs of the citizens, *not* from pulling wires behind the scene. But if it's going to work, we must be willing to in-

84

volve ourselves in the debate of issues, on every level. Fortunately, there's something you can do."

"What's that?" I said. I just don't seem to learn.

"Write a letter to the editor of your school paper, telling them what happened and what your proposal was."

"They wouldn't print it."

"You don't know that," Emily said, quite severe, "at least, until you try."

"I'm not much of a letter writer," I said. "In fact. I'm not much of a writer at all. I'm a better talker than a writer."

"Let's stick to writing," Emily said. "Being *good* isn't what's important. It's presenting the facts. How are the kids at Greeley High going to know what is going on around that school unless somebody tells them? So promise me you'll do it."

"I'll see."

"That's not good enough," Emily said. "You'll have to promise."

"Well, OK, then, I'll do it."

"Gee, Doug, thanks," said Emily, looking happy. "If that clerk wasn't watching I'd give you a kiss."

"I don't care if he's watching."

"I really only mean it figuratively," Emily said, getting down from the stool. "It isn't a good policy to mix business and pleasure."

"Then you do think you'd like it," I said, reaching for one of her hands. "I mean, you think you'd find it . . . find kissing a pleasure? Why don't we just go someplace and find out?"

"Douglas Radigan, you are impossible," said Emily, taking her hand away. "You go home and get that letter written.

We'll talk about that other later. And by the way, did you ask the clerk if he's for Senator Kieran?"

I shook my head.

"You must ask everybody," Emily said.

I waited at the front of the store while she got the poor guy to sign a support card and cough up some money from the cash register, then I walked her to Gabby's car. After that, there wasn't anything to do but go home.

It didn't help matters any that while I was waiting at an intersection for the lights to change, Curley Matthews came roaring up beside me. He leaned over, roared out the open window, "Go———yourself," then drove on, running a red light and leaving me in a pool of diesel fumes.

The first thing I noticed when I drove in the garage was that my dad's car was gone and that Norm's motorcycle was parked against the wall. Even so, I couldn't be sure that my dad had done what he'd threatened. Maybe he and my mother had gone out someplace before Norm came home.

I let myself in the back door without seeing anybody. In fact, it was so damned quiet that I walked softly, myself. Through the kitchen, dining room, and living room, and up the short flight of stairs that leads to the floor where all our bedrooms are. The door to my parents' bedroom was open, so was the door to Norm's. I could see a lot of his junk spread around on the bed, a sure sign he was home. My door was closed, however, and as I stood there I could hear someone moving around inside. Though I was practically sure it was Norm, I could still feel my flesh kind of crawl.

I opened the door fast and it was Norm. He was standing

86

by the window looking at the stuff inside one of the brown envelopes I'd gotten at Watt Tyler's house. He turned slowly. "You don't fall for all that crap, do you?"

Because of his beard, it's kind of hard to tell when Norm is smiling but I think he was. "It is crappola, you know."

"Maybe," I said. "But it's my crappola." I got hot very fast. "I don't even know what you're doing in my room, and with the door shut, at that."

"The wind blew it," Norm said, with this kind of sneer. He had a medallion on a leather thong around his neck and he swung it slowly around and around. "And as for what I'm doing in your room, I was looking for a package of cigarettes."

"I'm not about to commit suicide," I said. "I haven't smoked since I was twelve years old, and you know it."

"I thought maybe you'd started again. And I really was looking for cigarettes. Hopefully, for some grass, when I came across . . . this." He got up, letting the envelope drop as if it had already contaminated him. "It's got to go, Doug. It's no good. *He's* got to go. They all do. The President, Kieran, Frazier, that other monkey that's running—What's-His-Name—the lot of them. Maybe there was a time when somebody could have salvaged the country, but now it's too late. The old order, the old authority must be destroyed." There was a kind of glitter in Norm's eye that was almost scary. He wasn't just talking. He *believed* what he was saying. Just as Emily believed in Kieran's "new politics" of the people. And only one of them could be right.

"You're young, Doug. You haven't been around," Norm said, softly. "But in time you'll learn just how rotten, how corrupt our society is—that there has to be a new beginning."

87

"Get out of my room. Get out! I'll make up my own mind!"

Norm shrugged. "Whatever you say. It's your funeral." Taking his time, he walked out.

After he left, I lay down on my bed and stared at the ceiling until I heard Norm roar away on his motorcycle. Then I went downstairs. I'd told Norm I'd make up my own mind, and I had. If Emily ever discovered I hadn't canvassed the areas in my two brown envelopes, she'd never speak to me again. And while I was walking between the houses where I'd be knocking doors, I could think about the letter I'd promised to write to the school paper.

If I hadn't had that conversation with Norm just before I started out, I don't think that some of these places I saw and some of the people I talked to would have shook me up so. If he'd picked the two areas himself he just couldn't have put his point across any better.

In the first place, in the Manor district you don't walk between houses you drive. Most of them were at least a block apart, and set on lots so big that you couldn't see them from the street. Sometimes there were servants quarters and greenhouses, and always garages that would hold three cars, at least.

At the first house I came to, I stood out in front for five minutes before I got up nerve to ring the bell. Then nobody came. I was sure, though that I'd seen a curtain twitch at one of the windows and lights were on inside, all over.

At the next place, the maid who answered my ring said the family was in Florida and whatever it was that I was selling, she didn't want any.

I told myself if I got any more responses like those first

two that I was through. But I didn't. The man who came to the door listened as I gave my name. I told him that I was working for Senator Kieran and that I would appreciate him voting for the senator in the primary.

"I'm thinking rather seriously of doing that. Maybe this literature you have here will help me make up my mind."

He took the support card I gave him and said he might sign it later and if he did he'd send a check.

That was the closest I came to getting a vote for Kieran in the Manor district. Some people weren't home, or else didn't choose to come to the door. There was a gray Rolls parked in a graveled turnaround in front of one house, but when I got out just to look at it, a police dog the size of a pony came rushing out of the darkness and tried to take a bite out of my leg. Who they were for in that house, I never found out.

Everybody else I talked to was for The Man in the White House—who would be the man Kieran had to beat if he got the nomination. Which meant, I guessed, that they liked things the way they were. And why not, I thought, if you lived in a big house with servants, cars, (and police dogs), and all the money in the world?

I parked The Bomb under a street light and read the message on the second of my brown envelopes. "Twelfth Precinct, four blocks beginning East Fifteenth and Cooper, going north, both sides of the street."

I had to get a city map out of the glove compartment to find out where Cooper Street was.

One glance reminded me it lay between the city dump and the sewage disposal plant. The people who lived there called it The Bottoms.

In the summer I couldn't have stood it. But even with

89

snow on the ground and the temperature below freezing, it wasn't so good. I smelled it before I got there.

I don't think I ever thought very much about what hell would look like, but now I think it must look a little like the city dump. It stretched on and on for blocks. Fires burned here and there, lighting up the hulks of old cars, licking around their frames, flaring up, then dying down as small new flames appeared. For as far as I could see a kind of gassy curtain seemed to hang a few feet off the ground. Behind it, looking like a painted backdrop, were the lights of the city. The weather beacon on top of the First National Bank was white which mean it would be a clear day tomorrow.

A poor old bum came stumbling out of the darkness of the dump dragging a broken-down child's coaster wagon filled with junk.

Fifteenth and Cooper began at the corner. I drove the four blocks north slowly. There wasn't a shack I passed where I had the nerve to stop. In the flicker of the old-fashioned street lights, not like the new arc lights that had been put in almost everywhere else around town, I could see the junk-filled yards, the sagging porches, and the outhouses.

The Bomb's heater works fine, but even with it going full blast I began to shiver. It wasn't from the cold. Maybe Norm was right. Maybe there were two Americas, one for the rich and one for the poor. And maybe it was too late to do anything about it—except to tear the whole thing down and start over again.

In any case, somebody else would have to knock on doors in The Bottoms besides me. I turned The Bomb around and started home.

Before I left the freeway, my stomach began to grumble. And no wonder. It was after nine o'clock and all I'd had since lunch was a Coke. I took the exit which brought me out near school and The Strip. There I could take my choice of a pizza or a hamburger or, if Rubin's was still open, a pastrami on rye.

Although Pinky's was jumping as usual, Rubin had turned off the red neon "Delicatessen" sign in his window. Inside, however, one light was still on and I could see him, shirt-sleeves rolled up, starting to close for the night.

I tried the door and finding it locked, I knocked. He had to let me in. I know it was childish, but I suddenly felt that I had to have a pastrami on rye and if I couldn't have that, I didn't want anything at all. I knocked again.

Through the glass I could see him as he stood, head tipped, trying to decide whether or not to let me in. Then, wiping his hands on his long white apron, he walked up to the front of the store and turned the key in the lock.

"A hungry boy I should let in even if it is past closing hours. Yes? What is it you will have?" He walked behind the glass case that held the cold meats, the wheels and wedges of cheese, the lox, the kippered herring, a tray of big dill pickles.

I'd never noticed before how short Rubin was. All I could see of him as he stood behind the case was his head, bald and shiny, and his eyes peering out from behind a pair of old-fashioned steel glasses with wavy lenses.

I looked down into the case just as if I hadn't already made up my mind. "Pastrami. On rye."

He opened the sliding glass doors, took out the chunk of meat and carried it the length of the case to a wooden butcher's block at the end. I watched hungrily as he slipped

91

the meat into the jaws of the machine and slice after wafer-thin slice fell neatly down onto a piece of waxed paper. He really was giving me a lot. Then he turned, holding it out to me on the palm of his left hand. "This will be enough?"

"Fine, Mr. Rubin," I said. "Just fine." But I wasn't looking at the thin, pink slices of meat any more. A few inches up from the thumb on the soft, inner side of Mr. Rubin's arm was a row of numbers. Maybe three-eights of an inch high, they stood out cold and blue against the whiteness of his inner arm. I tried to take my eyes away and finding I could not, I closed them. I'd read about Hitler's concentration camps, of the millions that had died, of the few that had escaped.

"It's all right, son. Don't feel bad. Auschwitz is a long time ago. Almost thirty years. Now I fix your sandwich. On rye bread."

"I'm sorry anyway," I mumbled as Mr. Rubin buttered the thick slices of dark rye bread, spread mustard, and heaped on the pastrami. "You eat it here, or take it out?"

"I'll take it out," I said, though the truth was, I didn't want it at all. The inside of my mouth felt like it was lined with cotton.

"That will be eighty-five cents, plus two cents tax."

I paid, picked up the sandwich which Mr. Rubin had wrapped and put in a paper bag.

"Your change."

I was hoping he wouldn't notice it until I'd gone.

Even so, I should have left right then. Instead I blurted out, "It was bad . . . terrible what happened to you . . . your people. I mean, killing six million Jews . . . we'd never do anything like that. But right now in our country, things aren't so hot either." I was thinking about the old man coming out of the dump, "Rubin is a Jew Bastard," in dripping red paint, that rock somebody had thrown through his window a month before, the gray Rolls and the police dog. "My brother thinks that we should tear everything down and start over. Then it would be a better place for everybody."

Mr. Rubin shook his head. "No, son. It does not work like that. Getting rid of something bad—and there are some bad things in this country, yes, and in every country—but it doesn't mean something better will be put in its place. Violence is bad, always. In America we have good ways to improve. I learned about them when I became a citizen twenty years ago. And still I remember. We have the right to speak, to print our thoughts, to protest, to assemble peaceably and to vote—to elect our leaders." There was something shiny in Mr. Rubin's eye as he ticked them off on his fingers. "Yes, we have ways."

I'd forgotten the Kieran button on my jacket, until Rubin said, "Kieran, yes, we are for him, too. My wife and I both vote in every election—even the little ones—since we are citizens."

As he spoke, Mr. Rubin unlocked the door to let me out. And none too soon. Even through the brown paper bag the smell of the pastrami and rye bread had started getting to me. "Good night, my son. Come again soon," said Mr. Rubin. "Good night."

It was funny, only the day before it would have made me sore to have the little Jew call me his "son." Now I didn't mind. Before I reached The Bomb I was into the sandwich.

★ ★ ★ ★ ★ ★ ★

Chapter 8

☆ ☆ ☆ ☆ ☆ ☆ ☆

It took me most of the weekend to write the letter I'd promised Emily I'd send to the school paper. Even when I was in the study over the garage, I could hear my dad and Norm going at it. My dad hadn't left town after all, as he'd threatened to do, and as Norm didn't leave to go back to school until after a large Sunday dinner, they had time for a good workout.

For me, writing anything is hard work and I made about twenty false starts before I had a beginning. Then I got stuck again. It wasn't until I remembered Emily telling me I shouldn't worry about being a *good* writer, but that the important thing was to put down the facts. Tell the kids what had happened at the Student Council meeting. That got me going again, and when I'd finished I typed the whole thing out, making a carbon for Emily. A long time ago, my dad bought this big, old secondhand Underwood and though I use the Columbus method—discover and then land —my typing is still better than my writing. So the letter looked pretty good.

Monday after school I delivered it to the journalism

room. I hoped Monica wouldn't be there, but she was, looking at a copy of last week's paper spread out on one of the tables.

"Well, well," said Monica, taking in the envelope I had in my hand. "What do we have here? A messenger bringing the good news from Ghent to Aix? Whatever it is, you can give it to me."

"Thank you," I said, "but no thanks. It's for the editor."

"He's not here," Monica said, "but I can take care of it."

"You stick to your Club Notes," I said, "and I'll give my letter to What's-His-Name when I see him."

"The name's Meyer," somebody behind me said in a big, deep voice, but when I turned around the only person in sight was this skinny kid who came up about to my shoulder. He grinned. "Bernie Meyer. And I don't blame you for not giving whatever it is you've got there to that female vulture."

Monica looked pouty and said, "Oh, Bernie," and then went back to look at the paper again.

"It's a letter to the editor," I said. "So I thought I ought to give it to you. My name's Doug Radigan."

We then shook hands, which struck me as kind of silly, but then I hadn't acted like myself in weeks, so it didn't matter.

Bernie took the envelope, ripped it open, and read my letter through. First he grinned, but when he finished he wasn't looking so happy. "I don't suppose Burch will OK it. When I was made editor of the paper, I thought it was great. I was going to make over the school. But it doesn't work out that way when you've got a faculty advisor breathing down your neck every issue."

"Well," I said. "It was just a thought. I mean, I thought it was worth trying."

"Anything's worth trying," Bernie said, though he didn't sound as if he believed it. "Drop around again some time and we'll fan each other's flames."

Emily was sympathetic when I reported the conversation to her, but not sympathetic enough to go out with me on a date. The business about Mr. Rubin I kept to myself. And I didn't tell her, or anybody—Norm, least of all—how I felt when I'd canvassed the Country Club district and the streets that bordered the city dump. I just didn't want to talk about it. Working a little harder for Kieran, seemed to be the only sensible thing to do.

One day after school, at Emily's suggestion, I went down to spy on the other two candidates' headquarters. She said that the people who ran both Governor Frazier's and ex-Senator Swallow's campaign knew her and Gabby on sight, so they couldn't find out anything any more. But because I was still an "unknown"—I didn't care for that description too much, but I guess it was the truth—she said I might really find out how things were going for them.

What I found out didn't make me very happy. And that was, where the Kieran people pounced on every dollar bill that came into the office—the day somebody sent fifty bucks, Emily said, everyone went wild with joy—both Frazier and Swallow headquarters were loaded. The Frazier people had a corner location on the ground floor in the middle of downtown—some big store had just moved to the suburbs —and Swallow had space almost as good. Both had so much bunting and flags and campaign literature, you could hardly fight your way through either place.

96

At Kieran headquarters, you could hardly fight your way through the *kids*.

Sure, there were some kids at both places, but if you know what I mean, they just weren't with it. The important thing was, as I told Emily, both were over-confident. Each was so sure that his man was going to win, that they just weren't worrying.

Emily said that we would all have to work harder. So we did. Actually, as it got closer and closer to the primary, it got more exciting. A couple of times after school, I went in to talk to Watt Tyler, and I had one suggestion he thought was so good that he took it up with state headquarters and they decided to do it. It wasn't much, really. Just a piece of paper with a hole in it to slip over a doorknob if you went to call on somebody and you didn't find anybody home. Printed on it would be the words, "Senator Kieran called while you were out." After Kieran's name would be a star and down below another star where it would explain that it was a "worker" who had called. And, of course, it would give the date of the primary.

As a result, with all this going on, you could have knocked me down with a feather the day Miss Philbrick, who was still substituting for Miss Beckman in English, stopped me after class. She was smiling. "I just wanted to tell you, Douglas, that I thought your letter to the editor was excellent."

I did a double take. "But they didn't print it. The paper came out last Friday, and it wasn't in." I didn't like to admit that I'd cared, but I had gone over the paper about three times, looking to see if they might have used even part of it.

"But this is this week's paper," said Miss Philbrick. "It's

out a day early, on Thursday, because the shop that prints it is going to close for a long weekend to do some remodeling. Just a minute, I'll show it to you."

She nipped over to her desk, rummaged around under some stuff and came up with a copy of *The Tatler*. "It's on page two," she said, "right under the editorial."

I took the paper but something happened to my eyes when I tried to read. I saw the words "Student Says Council Undemocratic" at the top, and my name at the bottom of the page. But all the rest was a blur. I handed the paper back without saying anything. I was afraid my voice would split if I did.

Miss Philbrick is pretty little, and when she looked up at me she was smiling. "I will have to admit, Douglas, it did surprise me. The letter is very well done, and you must have spent a good deal of time on it. In any case, I am going to accept it in place of the Current Event's theme I asked the class to turn in on Monday. An 'A' on this piece of written work will improve your average quite a bit."

I mumbled thank you and got out of there in a hurry. I didn't feel sick, but I didn't feel so hot either. What I needed was air. And time to sort out my thoughts. So instead of going to my last class I went out and sat in The Bomb. There, I decided, my first and biggest mistake had been offering to help Watt Tyler get his car started. That one crummy "good deed" which really wasn't a good deed at all, but a pitch to get a better grade in American Government, had led me to the Kieran headquarters and Emily. And it was Emily who was responsible for everything else that had happened—even to writing the stupid letter that Miss Philbrick was going to give me an "A" on, which would improve my grade average, and thereby cause all kinds of complications. Already, I could hear my father growling, "If you brought your grades up in English and American Government, you could bring them up in your other studies, too."

At twenty minutes of four when kids started pouring out of the building, I went inside. I'd tried to convince myself that I didn't want a copy of the paper with my letter in it, but it was no go. I, at least, wanted to read it through, to see if it really was as good as Miss Philbrick said it was.

Monica was in the journalism room. Who else.

"Oh, hello," Monica said. "I rather thought you'd be stopping by. If you'd subscribed to the paper last fall as practically everybody in the whole of Horace Greeley High did, you'd not have to come crawling around asking for one."

"I'm not crawling around," I said. "If they're for sale, I'll buy one. If not, forget it."

"Be my guest," said Monica. She picked up a paper from a pile of them on a nearby table and handed it to me. "Maybe you would like several dozen so you could autograph them and give them to all your friends and relatives."

"I said to give me *one.*"

Monica looked sly. "I expect you know why your letter was printed."

In spite of myself, I went for the bait. "Why?"

"Because Mr. Burch is home sick, that's why."

I said I hoped it wasn't anything trivial but Monica pretended she hadn't heard. "Last week Bernie had it set in type, but Burch threw it out. But this week, when he's home sick, he slipped it in."

I said that with a back as broad as Burch's he could

have slipped in the sports section of the Cedar City *Sunday Clarion.*

"I think you enjoy being disgusting," said Monica.

I said, I did, then left—taking another copy of the school ᐧpaper with me.

I sat out in The Bomb and read my letter through about six times. Seeing it in print, not only made it look better but made it read better, too. It was hard to believe I'd written it. Maybe there were *two* Doug Radigans. Or maybe I had a split personality, like Dr. Jekyll and Mr. Hyde. If that was true, the bad side was a lot less trouble than the good side. Working on that theory, I decided I wouldn't tell Emily my letter had finally been printed in the paper. If I did, she'd immediately start dreaming up some new "good" thing for me to do.

I folded the two copies of the newspaper together and was stuffing them down inside a pocket of the car when I heard a tap at the window. It was Monica. A second later, she'd opened the door and popped inside. "You don't care if I sit here just a minute, do you, Douglas, until I get warm?"

"It wouldn't do me any good if I did care." I said. "You're already in."

"You hate me," said Monica, in a tiny voice, at the same time scrouging over on my half of the seat.

"I don't hate you either," I said, and at the moment it was true. Monica is a girl who has always smelled very good, and certain kinds of perfume really get to me.

"Yes, you do," said Monica. She pulled off one of my gloves and started moving my fingers back and forth.

"Listen, Monica," I said. "I *don't* hate you. I don't hate anybody. My motto is live and let live, you know that."
100

Monica was suddenly all smiles. "Then we're friends again! And to celebrate, I'm going to let you drive me home."

Monica lives practically in the next county, and by the time we got to her house, it was beginning to get dark. The minute we turned in the drive she reached over and turned off the ignition and said, "Douglas, kiss me. Just to prove that there are no hard feelings."

She gave me a smack, I gave her one, and we then sat there for about five minutes making out until Monica's father came out on the porch and said for her to get in the house that minute.

Monica sang out, "Coming, Daddy," to her father, and to me she said, "Saturday night, then, at eight. There's a dance at the Country Club."

"Hey!" I said. "Wait!" But I was too late. Monica was already gone.

When I got home, the phone was ringing. My mother was coming in from the kitchen to answer it, but I got there first.

It was Quig. He was so excited that for a minute I didn't recognize his voice. He let loose in a big, long spiel, the gist of which was a small revolution had taken place inside school last period. Of course, I'd been sitting out in The Bomb brooding and missed it all. Almost the minute the paper had been distributed, petitions had started circulating. By the time the bell rang, almost seven hundred kids had signed —about a third of the entire student body—and the petition had been presented to Mr. Burch, faculty advisor for the Student Council.

"The petitions demand that the cover I drew for the yearbook and the one drawn by the flack that Burch chose, be presented to the entire student body. And that the entire student body vote for the one of its choice.

"And all of this," Quig went on, "happened in a little more than an hour. I bet by this time tomorrow night, the kids circulating the petitions will have twice that many names. Right now, I think anything could happen. And it's because of you, Doug, and your letter."

I just kind of pawed the ground, saying the letter wasn't all that good and that I hadn't really done anything, but Quig wouldn't buy it. He said that my letter had hit the majority of kids right where they live. "You see," he said, "they know that you're not a wheel but just an ordinary guy. In fact, they've never heard of you. That's where your strength lies. In a way, you're like your friend, Senator Kieran. Nobody had ever heard of him except a handful of people, until he got so fed up with the professional politicians running the country—and running it into the ground —that he decided to try for the nomination, himself."

I guess any guy who doesn't like to hear himself praised, must have a screw loose somewhere. And I liked hearing Quig saying what he did—even to comparing me with Senator Kieran—although I knew he was exaggerating plenty.

The next morning when I went to school, however, I was hardly inside the building when this skinny kid with big ears came running up to me. "Signed the petition yet?" he said, at the same time handing me a couple of sheets of paper stapled together and a ball-point pen. Typed on the first sheet was something like, "We, the undersigned, demand that the entire student body of Horace Greeley High be allowed to pass on the cover of the yearbook." The rest of the sheet was covered on both sides with signatures, and the second sheet was almost half-filled.

102

"Sure," I said, "I'll sign it." I wrote "Doug Radigan" and handed it back to him.

"You're Doug Radigan?"

The kid was so bug-eyed, I couldn't help grinning. "In person."

"Gol!" the kid said. "Did you ever start something! Wait until I tell Leona!"

If I'd wanted to, I could have signed fifty more petitions. Between periods, kids were running around everywhere, shoving them under people's noses. Even during class, I could see sheets of paper being passed around. Kids I didn't know spoke to me in the halls. And in American Government Watt Tyler made a little speech about me.

My ears were burning so I could hardly listen, but what the words all added up to was that every single individual can affect the political system, and that political systems exist not only on the national, state, county, and city levels, but in labor unions, school organizations, everywhere. "So don't overlook the legitimate, democratic avenues open to you," he wound up, "always remembering . . ." He paused, then walked up to the blackboard, picked up a stubby piece of chalk. "I think maybe you'd better copy this in your notebooks." Then he wrote, "The Far Left and the Far Right are both totalitarian. They are both Fascist." He turned around. "Anybody care to comment? Douglas, you?"

I shook my head. I couldn't have commented if I'd wanted to.

Quig was waiting for me at my locker after school. He said, that, so far fourteen hundred and seventy-two kids out of a total enrollment of two thousand and twenty-five, had signed petitions. A lot *hadn't* signed because they were afraid they'd get in trouble, but thought the petition was a

103

good idea and they'd like to vote on the cover if they had a chance.

"We're going to give the kids one more day to get names, and then Bernie Meyer and I are going to present the rest of the petitions to Burch. It's a victory whether we win or not."

Quig's final words didn't make much sense, but that seemed to be about par for the course any more. I rode around in The Bomb for a while, trying to remember how things had been before. How great it was when my only problem was trying to decide whether I'd buy a Maserati, a Mach II, or a Bossa Nova—after I'd found the cache of Inca gold in the Andes. But The Bomb's magic didn't seem to be working. Instead of a magic, there was a kind of grinding noise in the gears I'd never heard before.

When I came up from the garage my mother had dinner ready. The phone rang, though, before I could sit down. It was Emily and she was excited. Someone had brought a copy of the school paper down to headquarters and she'd seen my letter. She also heard about the petitions. Her voice had a little quiver in it. "Douglas, I'm *proud*." Even under my wool pullover, I could feel goose bumps on my arms. I wondered how I could ever have wanted her *not* to know about the letter.

"It's all because of you," I mumbled.

"No, you," Emily said, and the goose bumps started coming up again. For about two minutes after that, neither one of us said anything, there was just this very nice kind of breathy silence. Then Emily said, the next important thing to discuss was the trip to the River Cities in the western part of the state that hadn't had sufficient exposure to the

104

Kieran message. So a crew was going there from Cedar City. Several of the other larger cities in the state were also sending teams.

"Our bunch will leave at the crack of dawn Saturday morning. Somebody will find a place for us to stay that night, and we'll come back to Cedar City late Sunday. Mr. Tyler's taking his VW bus, so you won't need to drive."

I said I'd have to make some arrangements but I thought I could go, all right, and Emily hung up. I was also thinking how great it would be to be around Emily with both arms free.

My mother was waiting for me when I got back to the table. She hadn't started to eat. One good thing about her, though, she never bugs me when she thinks I'm talking to a girl on the phone.

"Monica?" she said, smiling.

Suddenly, I felt this dead weight lying at the bottom of my stomach. "M . . . Monica?"

"Yes," my mother said. "I think it's so nice you two children are going together again. Her mother was in the store today and told me. I guess girls confide in their mothers more than boys do. But that's all right, dear. I just pretended that I knew. Monica's mother said she's always preferred you over all the other boys Monica's gone out with. She said she never could stand that Rodney Van Pratt that Monica broke up with last weekend."

I put my fork back on my plate and pushed back my chair.

"Douglas!" my mother said. "Is something wrong? You don't look well at all."

I didn't answer her.

Maybe it was chicken, but I couldn't bring myself to tell Monica to her face that I wasn't going to take her to the dance at the Country Club. So I wrote her a letter. What else? With *my* reputation.

Even so, I won't say I didn't sweat over it. Although it was mostly Monica's fault, I'd given some kind of consent by sitting in the car and making out with her. It took me most of the evening before I had a draft that I thought would pass, then I sneaked some of my mother's notepaper that's got a lot of bluebirds and flowers on it and an envelope, and copied it—it was then down to four lines—in my best handwriting, which is still pretty bad.

This is what it said: "Dear Monica: I am sorry I cannot take you to the dance on Saturday night, but Senator Kieran has requested that I be a member of a task force to cover the River Cities of Bluffs, Council Rock, and Apache this weekend. For the sake of my country, this must take priority." I played with the idea of signing it, "Ask not what your country can do for you, but what you can do for your country," but finally decided plain, "patriotically" was safer. So that is what I did.

Chapter 9

☆ ☆ ☆ ☆ ☆ ☆ ☆

WHAT I REALLY wanted to do was mail the letter, but I wasn't quite that big a heel.

When Monica and I had been going steady I'd known her schedule as well as my own, so I was waiting when she came out of the cafeteria at noon.

"Oh, Douglas! I was just hoping I would see you." Monica looked very happy and excited until I took the letter out of my notebook and handed it to her. "What's this?"

"A letter," I said. "For you. But now I've got to be going."

"Oh, no, you don't," Monica said, taking me by the arm. "I don't know why you should be writing me a letter at all, unless there's something you don't want to *tell* me."

"Not necessarily. I've got to go. Right now."

Monica had ripped open the envelope and read the letter before I could take a step. "I knew it! I positively knew it! And blaming it on Senator Kieran. Saying it's for the good of your country! I don't know what's come over you. You've changed . . . you're different . . . you're not the same person at all."

107

At first, I'd thought Monica was going to hit me but by the time she finished, she'd taken a step backward and was looking at me very narrowly as if she expected me to change still more. "In the future, I will thank you to stay completely away from me, until you can act like yourself again."

With that, she flounced off leaving me in the center of a little knot of kids who'd gathered to watch the excitement.

I got one break I hadn't expected. My folks decided to go away for the weekend. The great thing about the arrangement was that I hadn't yet figured out how to break the news that I planned to be out of town, too.

By the time they were ready to leave Friday night, I had enough instructions to land a man on Mars. Not only was I to water the house plants, bring in the milk, check the humidifier and leave a note for the milkman but I was to wind an eight-day clock that had come West with my great-great-grandfather Radigan in a covered wagon. God.

Instead, as soon as my folks were out of the house I went down to Kieran headquarters to see Emily. When I told her about the petitions, she cried, "Douglas!" and though I thought for a moment she was going to kiss me, she wound up by saying that was a perfect example of democracy at work, and she hoped I had learned a valuable lesson from it.

After that, we spent about two hours going over precinct lists for the River Cities, and cutting them up into sections to be handed out to the various workers.

I drove Emily home but she was out of the car before I could turn off the ignition. From a safe distance she called out, "Headquarters at 7 A.M.," and that was it.

108

I was there at five minutes of seven, and except for one spot for me Watt Tyler's VW bus was already full. Naturally, the empty seat wasn't next to Emily. Red Beard sat beside her—rather closer than necessary.

The rest of the people I already knew. Gribbles, looking Ivy League even at 7 A.M., Betty Stringfellow, Dodie Pembroke—who at first I didn't recognize because since I'd seen her last she'd had the baby—Mike Bridges and Pete D'Mario, a kid I really liked and who, reportedly, was related to almost every restaurant owner in Cedar City.

Counting Watt Tyler, Emil, Red Beard, and me that made eight of us, and by the time we got to the outskirts of the River Cities, pressure had built up inside the bus until you could almost feel its sides begin to swell.

Red Beard told us to simmer down until we got to head-quarters where we would get specific instructions. As it turned out, however, that was just our first step. From there, we were sent to an empty-store building in an outlying shopping center that had been set up as a sort of command post to instruct workers as they arrived.

Inside the building, it was organized chaos. Kids were falling all over each other, phones were ringing, and a guy with a loudspeaker was standing on a desk telling people where to go.

We hunted around until we found a sign that said Sand-hill—that was our city—where we found a couple of ladies handing out precinct lists and mimeographed maps. A little further along, we were given envelopes filled with cam-paign material.

As two or three carloads of kids took off, three or more carloads arrived. Somebody else had gotten himself a mega-

109

phone and was bawling out that in case of doubt, workers were either to phone in or come back to headquarters. Not a single name on a single list was to be missed. Beller, beller. Between twelve and one o'clock, food trucks with free sandwiches and hot drinks would visit the different areas. Beller, beller again. Sleeping arrangements for all workers were being made and would be assigned later. He wound up with a loud, "All right, kids, let's blitz it!" then like a phonograph record started in at the beginning again.

Less than a half hour passed, however, before our crew was all back in Mr. Tyler's VW bus and headed for Sandhill. Every dozen blocks or so he'd drop some kids off. Pretty soon there were only four of us left. Gribbles, D'Mario, Emily, and me. Then Mr. Tyler dropped us, and that was it.

It's kind of hard to explain, but this time knocking doors was different. Before it had been a sort of game. This time it really mattered. Part of the reason, I think, was that the election was only a few days away. Mostly, it was because I knew that Kieran really had a chance. The last state-wide public opinion poll showed that for the first time Kieran was really gaining. Watt Tyler said there wasn't a doubt but what the Frazier people were worried, and if the Swallow people weren't worried, they should be.

Not once, that whole day, did I ever feel that I was wasting my time. Sure, there were boo-boos. Funny things happened. I mean, for example, how would you like to march up to somebody's front door, ring the bell, and after a quick look at your precinct list to be sure you had the right name, have this scene take place.

Doug: Mrs. Smith?

Lady: I'm not Mrs. Smith.

110

Doug (taking another quick glance at his list): Are you sure Mrs. Aretha Smith doesn't live here?

Lady: Young man, I'm quite sure. My name is Mrs. Oliver.

Doug (desperately): *Did* Mrs. Smith . . .

Lady: Young man, I've lived in this house for the last twenty-seven years. Good-bye. (door shuts)

Doug (now in real desperation, rings bell bringing lady to door one more time): Mrs. Oliver, I'm working for Senator Kieran and I . . .

Lady: Good heavens, boy, why didn't you say so in the first place? Come into the house this minute and get warm.

It helped, too, that the weather was nice. Cold, but the sun was shining and most people in the area had shoveled their sidewalks after the last snow so walking wasn't bad. I guess it was a neighborhood you'd call middle class. Maybe *middle* middle class. On most houses there was a television aerial. Some people were gardeners and grew roses. Like my dad, they'd tied up their climbers in burlap bags. And being Saturday, there were lots of kids around. And dogs. A big old dog that I guessed to be about half Newfoundland and half Labrador would be following me yet if I hadn't taken him back to the house on whose porch he'd been sitting when I saw him first.

Mostly, too, our lists were accurate. And while a lot of people had already made up their minds how they were going to vote an awful lot were still on the fence. It was with the undecided ones that the time spent really counted.

What's really funny is that lots of times the fact that we were kids and that we weren't "getting anything out of it" was what made the difference.

Then why are you doing it, people would ask? And I'd

111

answer saying that kids liked Senator Kieran because he was honest. That he didn't say just the things people wanted to hear but things he really believed.

The time passed so fast that I had to hurry to get back to the corner where I was supposed to meet D'Mario, Emily, and Gribbles at twelve o'clock.

D'Mario was already there, and although pretty soon Gribbles and Emily arrived from different directions the food truck didn't. We waited for it until about a quarter of one then went back to our lists. D'Mario was the only one who grumbled. If a D'Mario were delivering it, he said, it would *be* there.

I didn't get back to the corner again until after six o'clock. Parked under a street lamp, I could see Mr. Tyler's VW bus and at that point, it looked better to me than any Maserati.

Mr. Tyler rolled down the window when he saw me coming. "You haven't got Emily there, have you?"

I shook my head.

"We've got everybody but her."

The door was open to the bus, but I didn't get in. I hadn't been cold all day, but suddenly I was cold all over.

"Get in, Doug. And don't worry. We'll find her."

"You look for her," I said. "I'll stay here in case she comes." I'd talked so much that day I was croaking.

From inside the bus, a voice as cracked as my own said, "Here she comes now. Or, at least it looks like her."

It was Emily. I could see the white blur of her face and her silly white boots shining in the darkness. I ran to meet her.

"Good luck?"

112

"Good luck."

I took her mittened hand.

Watt Tyler had turned the bus around by the time we got to the corner. Two people moved over and made places for us. After that, there was a lot of talking as we all compared experiences. Then, except for hungry stomachs grumbling, there was silence.

From the driver's seat, Watt Tyler laughed softly. "I think somebody's trying to tell me something. Just have patience. It won't be long before we'll find out where you kids are going to lay your weary heads tonight, and we've got to get some food inside those empty stomachs."

I knew our first stop was the store building where we'd been that morning, but it seemed a long time before we got there. When we did, Mr. Tyler was the only one who went in and almost a half hour elapsed before he came out.

"I guess we've got a place, but the line was always busy when they phoned. But these people—the Gundersons— volunteered a couple of days ago to sleep a bunch of kids— so I guess we'll have to take them at their word."

"Are they going to feed us?" It was D'Mario.

Mr. Tyler said he couldn't take a chance on that so we stopped at the next McDonalds where everybody wolfed down hamburgers and shakes.

The result of this was that it was after nine o'clock by the time Mr. Tyler again stopped the bus. The street sign at the corner said McPherson Avenue. The number painted on a rock at the curb was 3719—the Gundersons' address— the porch light was on and there were three cars in the drive. But still there had to be some mistake. If each of the three cars represented only two people (unlikely), and if there were two Gundersons (at least) there simply wasn't going to be room to sleep eight people more—all of them except Emily and Betty rather large—in that smallish story-and-a-half house.

Mr. Tyler, himself, didn't sound too confident. "Maybe I'd better go in first—to see if they're expecting us. Doug, you come, too."

I followed him up the driveway and on the porch and tried to smile reassuringly as we waited for someone to answer. It would be cold sleeping in the bus all night, but I had begun to think that even sounded good by the time the door finally opened. The woman was a good deal older than my mother. That surprised me. I guess I thought anybody who'd put up a bunch of kids working for Kieran would be young, themselves.

But she was surprised, too. "Two more?" she said with a little quiver. Then she laughed. "We're already sleeping eight. I was just up in the attic getting out the children's old sleeping bags. So we might as well make it ten. Come on in."

Mr. Tyler had started backing away before she finished her sentence. Then he laughed. "There aren't just two of us. There are six more in the bus."

The woman put her hand up under her gray curly bangs, then turned and called back in the house. "Ralph! Come quickly! I think I'm going to faint!"

I saw a man that I guessed was her husband coming on the double but before he got to the door she was apologizing. "I'm not going to faint, really. We'll manage. Go get your kids and tell them to come in. We will make do, somehow."

And they did. I don't yet know how. By ten thirty, not

counting the Gundersons or their own three teen-age kids who had gone off to their own rooms—there were sixteen people sleeping in that house. Almost every square foot of space in the living room and dining room had a body in it. Some kids had brought their own sleeping bags. These were veterans of other primary campaigns, Watt Tyler told me. Older, more serious and quiet, I guess maybe they set the standard for the rest of us. There just wasn't any horsing around. Mrs. Gunderson supplied blankets or sleeping bags to kids who didn't have any, and there were stacks of washcloths and hand towels in the first-floor bathroom and a shower stall off a family room in the basement. There was a couple of gallons of coffee in huge pots in the kitchen, and stuff to make sandwiches for the kids who hadn't eaten. I had a little something more, listened to news on TV, then went looking for Emily.

I found her in the family room downstairs, rolled up in an army blanket underneath the Ping-Pong table. The light shining in from the hall at the foot of the basement stairs at which I stood was dim and, at first, I saw only her head. Then she spotted me, and sitting up, beckoned. I stepped over the sleeping shape of Mr. Tyler, likewise wrapped up in a blanket with his head on a sofa cushion, and the bodies of three or four other kids I'd never seen before.

"I saved you a place," Emily said, sleepily, she flopped down again. "This is really great under here. No one can step on you."

Mrs. Gunderson had run out of blankets but she'd given me an old bedspread that she said her kids had always taken to camp. It smelled of poison-ivy lotion, wood smoke, and chocolate candy bars.

I wrapped myself up carefully, leaving my arms out, and crawled in under the table.

"Golly," Emily said, still dreamily. "You smell like . . . you smell like . . ."

"Camp," I said. "But never mind that." After pursuing Emily for nearly six weeks and having her alone at last, even if it was under a Ping-Pong table with a dozen or so other people lying about—I didn't want to talk about camp.

One of Emily's hands was lying out on top of her sleeping bag, and I think I might have held it if I tried. But I had a different plan, to roll a quarter turn toward her, then throw my arm out as if I were asleep, then very, very slowly inch it in under her head and shoulders.

Around the room, in different keys, came a variety of snores, and a few soft "poohs" from the girls.

I managed the quarter turn. Light from a street light outside was now shining through one of the small high windows of the room. Emily's face looked pure, ghostlike, and very beautiful. I can't explain it, but it was nice just looking at her.

And that's how I missed out on the best opportunity I'd ever had to kiss Emily Marlow or even hold her hand. The next thing I knew it was morning.

★ ★ ★ ★ ★ ★ ★

Chapter 10

☆ ☆ ☆ ☆ ☆ ☆ ☆

It was a little after seven o'clock Sunday evening when Watt Tyler dropped me in front of Kieran headquarters in Cedar City.

I'd left The Bomb in an alley behind the building, and as I walked toward it I could see a sheet of paper tucked under the windshield wiper.

I lifted the blade of the wiper and resisting the temptation to rip the traffic ticket into shreds, stuffed it in my pocket. I was sore. Cops ought to have more to do than prowl around in patrol cars, in alleys, for God's sake, looking for cars that might be parked illegally. I knew without looking that "The Shadow" had written it. So I took it out of my pocket and looked at it, and sure enough, the initials scrawled at the bottom were W. M.

I can tell you, it didn't do anything to improve my mood. To begin with, the neighborhood which we'd started canvassing that morning right after the Gundersons had fed us, just wasn't a Kieran neighborhood. At least, three out of every five people I talked to said they were going to vote for

Frazier in the primary. In some blocks it was four out of every five. The day before, it had been just the other way around. A few, even, were for that racist, Swallow.

Not only did the rest of our crew report the same kind of results, other kids that we bumped into out canvassing were as discouraged as we were. The day before, I think, we would all have agreed that Kieran had better than an even chance to come out ahead in the primary. By Sunday evening when we started back, I wouldn't have bet a worn-out Beatle record for his chances.

Besides that, I'd hardly had a chance to say a word to Emily all day. To finish it all, as we'd reached the edge of Cedar City, Mr. Tyler said that he would drive anybody home who hadn't left his own car at headquarters. I said that I'd be glad to drive Emily home, but he said, no, that tomorrow was a school day—God—and he wanted everybody settled in his own bed as soon as possible. And that was that.

Driving home it all began to multiply. If Kieran *did* lose, just where would I be? And the answer was, nowhere at all.

Not that I was any political expert, but I'd listened to Watt Tyler, Red Beard, Emily, and some of the other pros around headquarters long enough to get the picture. If Kieran won the primary in our state, he'd go into the California primary as a strong candidate for the nomination. If either Frazier or Swallow won, Kieran would no longer be a viable—that was their word, not mine—in the California primary. If Kieran lost again in California, he was through.

And if Kieran was through, so was I. Headquarters would close, Emily would disappear. I'd have no place to go to and nothing to think about. School, which lately had become bearable because of Watt Tyler and Miss Philbrick would go back to being a pain in the butt again.

Because my mind was wandering, I was driving slowly. So it was pretty ridiculous when I saw that the car behind, which could have passed me, didn't pass. Then I saw it was a police car, the spinner unlighted, and that the big square shape humped over the wheel belonged to "Shadow" Morrison.

To be certain he was really following me, I speeded up. He did, too. When I slowed, he still stayed the same distance behind.

I slipped onto the freeway at the posted speed, left it two exits later, backtracked and got back on it. In the next ten minutes I was on and off another couple of times and "Shad" was still with me. It began to get funny. The poor, dumb dope. Who did he think he was fooling? The intelligence of cops must be just about what Norm had always said it was. And if Norm was right about that, he might be right about the brutality bit. I remembered, too, Norm saying as long as a month ago that Kieran didn't have a chance, that working for him was nothing more than an exercise in futility. Norm did have a way of saying things, sometimes.

As soon as I decided to shake "Shad," I did and a few minutes later when I exited onto The Strip he was nowhere in sight. But Curley Matthews was. I hadn't seen him since the night he'd insulted me while I was waiting at the intersection for the lights to change. To avoid anything like that happening again, I turned in the direction opposite the one Curley was headed. Not that I'm chicken, but I just didn't think I could take anything off of him after what I'd been through the last couple of days. But it wasn't any use. A second later, he had made a U turn and had come up on the left side of The Bomb forcing it into the curb.

I get mad fast and it took everything I had not to grab a

119

handful of Curley's long, straight hair, yank him out of his car, and beat him to a pulp.

Instead, I took a long deep breath. "Ten seconds to get that crate out of my way," I growled. "And I've started counting."

"Oh, me! How very fierce!" Curley pretended to cringe. "And all I wanted was to see if you wanted to drag. Or maybe you've given up dragging, along with women. Except for that washed-out blonde you've been running around with, and she don't count."

And that did it.

Curley drew in his head, like a turtle going back into its shell. As he jammed his foot on the diesel's accelerator, I jammed mine down on The Bomb's.

I caught up with him as we crossed the bridge over the freeway, switched lanes so I was on his left, then almost fender to fender we took the diagonal that runs into The Avenue, the main highway that runs through Cedar City.

Then, while I was slowing for a couple of oncoming cars to pass so I could push the throttle to the floor, it happened. I didn't see it, but behind me I heard the scream of brakes, the crunch and grind of metal, a deafening thud of impact.

I pulled The Bomb to the curb and got out. Almost a block behind me I could see the snapped off telephone pole and the wreckage of the diesel, its headlights turned crazily skyward. From far off, I heard the wail of sirens, and seconds later saw the revolving red lights from a patrol car's spinner.

I got back in The Bomb and started for home. There wasn't anything I could do for Curley. Alive or dead. And there was plenty that going back there could do to me.

The closer I got to Paradise Acres, the uneasier I got. And

it wasn't just the accident. I can't explain it. I just had this feeling that something more was about to go wrong.

The minute I turned onto our street I could see that the lights in our house were on. So my folks were home ahead of me. That was it. The clock would have stopped, the newspapers would still be on the doorstep, and the milk not brought in. For a nickel I would have kept on going and never come back. When I opened the garage door and saw that my dad's car wasn't there after all, I knew that was what I should have done. The sweet and heavy smell of pot had penetrated even to the garage and in the house it was worse. I opened a window in the kitchen, pushing back the storm to let in some fresh air. The sink had a couple of dirty skillets in it and a bunch of eggshells Norm had been too lazy to push down the garbage grinder. The counters were loaded with dirty glasses and plates. Either Norm had been hungrier than usual, or he'd been feeding some of his friends.

The living room was a mess, too. The ash trays were full of cigarette stubs mixed in with little twisted butts of grass. Potato chips were mashed into the carpet and there were more dirty dishes.

Upstairs, Norm's bed had been slept in and left unmade. Mine was the same. I ripped off the sheets and pillowcases and stuffed them down the clothes chute. I knew I wasn't going to sleep on *them*.

Back in the kitchen, I took in the milk and while the dishwasher worked on the plates and glasses, I wound and started the clock and opened more windows. In the living room I dumped the ash trays and emptied the wastebasket which was full to overflowing with wads of paper. While running the vacuum I came across another piece. Scarcely crumpled, I could tell at a glance that the handwriting that

121

covered it belonged to Norm. He's the only person in the world whose handwriting is worse than mine. At the top of the page were the words "Master Plan." If I hadn't already been so sore at him, I would have laughed. A Master Plan for the revolution, no doubt. And while he and his friends were planning it, they were sitting around stuffing themselves with food my folks' hard work had paid for. And sleeping in *my* bed.

Through the front window I could see the headlights of a car flash in our drive and for a minute I panicked, but the car had only been turning around and I went on cleaning.

By nine o'clock, I'd finished the downstairs and went around and shut the windows. I could no longer tell how the place smelled, but the house was getting cold so I turned up the heat.

When I got upstairs, I made Norm's bed and got clean sheets for my own, then checked the bathroom. But I needn't have worried about that. Norm doesn't shave, neither do his friends. I guess they don't take showers either because the bath towels were as neat as my mother had left them.

I took a quick shower myself, then headed for the sack. I hadn't been there ten minutes before I heard the garage door go up and then come down again. The folks were home.

Although I was listening, my mother came upstairs so quietly I didn't hear her until she opened the door to my room and said, "Douglas, dear, are you asleep?"

I thought about it, then said, "Yes."

My mother laughed. "Is everything all right?"

I said, "Yes," again.

"That's good," my mother said. "Though I did think the house smelled a little funny."

122

I let that one pass.

"Did Norm get home?"

I made a noise that could have meant "yes."

My mother took it that way. "I'm glad. After all, it *is* his home. And he has as much right here as anybody. No matter what your father says."

"Sure," I said. "Sure, he does."

I thought maybe then she'd go away. But she didn't. A little light came in from a street lamp outside, and I could see her shape outlined against a piece of wall.

"We would have been home sooner," my mother said, "except for the accident."

There is this thing about my mother. She knows how to get your attention even if you're trying to go to sleep.

"Not you and Dad?" I said.

"Oh, my goodness, no! Your father is an excellent driver. I've never known him to take a chance. But if we'd come home the way we always do, we would have missed it all. But for some reason, your father instead of taking the freeway all the way out to Paradise Acres decided to come home by way of The Avenue."

I'd been lying on my stomach but I turned on my side so I couldn't hear my heart thumping.

"It really was a terrible accident. Two kids had been drag racing. One made it across—but the other one . . ." My mother shuddered, then went on. "I guess they didn't know, but a policeman had been following them. He saw this boy trapped in the car—your father said that when the fire started, if it had been an ordinary car that uses gasoline, both the policeman and the boy would have been burned to death. . . ."

123

"They . . . They're all right?"

"The boy was unconscious, but the policeman got him out of the car before the fire got out of control. Your father said that the policeman shouldn't have risked his life diving into the flames to risk his life for some punk kid, but he did. His . . . his clothes were burned off." My mother covered her eyes. "Traffic was so tied up we couldn't leave until after the ambulances came. . . ." My mother's voice was shaking.

"Don't think about it," I said.

My mother came over to the bed, felt me out and kissed my forehead, then went out and closed the door.

By morning, I knew one thing. And that was that I wasn't going to school. I heard my folks stirring around before it was light and when my mother came in my room to get me up I told her I was sick.

"I knew I shouldn't have left you alone this weekend," she said. "I love your Aunt Rita and Uncle Ralph, but the trip just wasn't worth it."

I told her I'd be all right if she'd just go away and leave me alone.

"Gladly," said my mother. "But please don't bite my head off." She went away then and pretty soon I heard her and my father leave for work.

I really didn't feel so hot. I'd had a hard time going to sleep and when I finally did I dreamed about "The Shadow." That he died. Curley wasn't in it—the dream, I mean—and that was the only good thing about it. Apart from that, I couldn't help thinking what would happen when the doctor said that Curley was getting along well enough to talk to reporters and police.

I went downstairs to get the morning paper. It was in the

kitchen where my dad had eaten breakfast and was neatly put back together again.

The story was on page one, with a big headline over it saying "Police Officer Pulls Boy from Burning Car. Condition Critical. Seek Driver of Fleeing Car." There was a picture of what was left of Curley's diesel.

I read the story through and it wasn't much different from the way my mother had told it. There were two things, though, that nobody knew. One, that I was the driver of the missing car and that "Shadow" Morrison wouldn't have been anywhere near the site of the accident unless he'd been trailing me. And if the poor, dumb dope died that, in a way, would be my fault, too.

The poor, dumb dope. The label didn't fit any more. I'd always said "Shad" hated kids, too. But a cop who hated kids wouldn't risk his neck to save somebody who hated his guts the way Curley did.

I went back to bed and tried to go to sleep but it was no go. A little later I got up, dressed, and went to school.

It would have been better if I'd stayed home. About the middle of the afternoon, my head started aching and my throat felt as if it was lined with sandpaper. Though I did manage to last out what was left of the day Mr. Tyler, who I bumped into in the washroom just before fifth period, told me I looked like the walking wounded and to go home and stay there until I felt better. "And don't come near headquarters, either," he added. "Kieran doesn't need to add the names of any martyrs to his credentials."

After that, I was out of it for four or five days. On Tuesday and Wednesday my mother stayed home from work and I

125

was even too sick to care when she asked Dr. Yarrow to come and see me. The last time I'd seen him was when I was thirteen and he'd given me a bunch of shots before I went to Y camp. He gave me a shot this time, too, and left a prescription for some pills that my mother came running around every four hours to see that I swallowed.

My mother thought I was out of my head when I kept asking all the time to see the newspapers. For a while, I think I really had been kind of delirious or something because I had this hang-up that if Morrison died, I'd die, too. By Saturday, however, he was still alive and although extensive skin grafts would have to be made, hope was held for his recovery. Curley had regained consciousness and though doctors believed he had sustained no serious injury, he was still not believed to be in any condition to be questioned by the police. After that, I took a good deep breath and went on reading everything I could find on the election—Senator Kieran had made a number of appearances around the state and had been mobbed by kids and young people—then I'd sleep some more.

Sunday morning when I woke up, however, I felt almost human and while my folks were at church I called Emily at headquarters. I hadn't talked to her since the Sunday night a week before when we drove home from the River Cities.

She asked if my mother had told me she'd called a couple of times to see how I was, and I said she had. It seems a lot of other people were sick, too. Neither D'Mario nor Red Beard had been in all week, and Gribbles had said he felt as if he was coming down with the bubonic plague.

Emily didn't sound too hot, herself, but I think that was mostly discouragement. Somebody had been going around

126

all over town, she told me, tearing down Kieran posters and signs but that neither Frazier or Swallow stuff had been disturbed.

I said maybe we ought to go around and tear down a few of their signs and she said, "Douglas! You don't mean that!" in this real shocked voice so I had to say I didn't mean it.

"They have so much money, too," Emily went on. "They're just pouring it into this primary—and we're so poor we've scarcely money to buy postage stamps."

"Listen," I said. "I'm coming down."

"No, Douglas, you mustn't. I'm all right, really, except for being a little low. It's just when I think about Kieran losing, having to wait another four years before we can try again . . . think about going back to school and leaving everybody . . . Gabby, Mr. Tyler, Gribbles . . ."

"And me?"

"And you. . . ."

"Most of all?" My throat filled up so I could hardly talk.

Emily laughed. Softly. But she was laughing. "Douglas Radigan, you are impossible. But I've got to hang up. Another phone is ringing."

I could hear it ringing myself, so I knew she really had to go.

After that, I went back to bed. By morning, I had to feel good enough to get going again. I decided that both Emily and Kieran needed me.

It turned out, Emily didn't need me quite as much as I'd hoped for. Though she did give me credit for a hundred-dollar check that had come in the mail that morning. It was sent by—you'd never guess—that rich guy in the Manor

127

District who'd said he'd give some money if he decided to vote for Kieran. Emily showed me the note that came with the check, saying he had been impressed by the young man who had called on him. Impressed with *me*. That was a new one.

After that, we didn't get to talk much because the place started swarming with new workers, mostly kids who'd been turned on by a recent Kieran speech, that had come in loud and clear, in favor of lowering the voting age to eighteen. The kids had come to distribute door hangers—my idea—saying "Kieran Cares, VOTE on Tuesday." Ten thousand of them. Ye Gods. It was almost enough to make me forget about "Shad" and Curley.

Every two seconds the telephone rang—people calling in to say they needed a ride to the polls, or who wanted to talk to Red Beard or Mr. Tyler about some last minute strategy. Ladies called, too, asking if they should bring cookies or a cake to the victory celebration at headquarters the next night.

I took one of the "cake-cookies" telephone calls and had to ask Emily which one.

"Cookies," Emily said. "Less mess."

I said, "Cookies. Less mess," to the lady on the telephone. Then it hit me.

I turned to Emily. "What if Kieran loses and we don't have a victory celebration?"

"All the more reason to eat," Emily said. I knew she was trying to make a joke but it didn't come off. If Kieran lost, nobody would be able to eat at all.

The things I learned you'd never believe. I mean, for example, in some states in a primary election if you're a

128

registered Republican you can only vote for a Republican candidate—likewise, if you're a Democrat—unless you go to the trouble of changing your registration well ahead of the election. In our state, it's not like that. You can vote for whomever you choose.

So you could have knocked me over with a feather the next morning when my mother, who doesn't always vote, said she was going to vote for Kieran, and asked if I'd drive her to the polls before she went to work. "Your father voted absentee." She didn't say for whom, but I guessed for Frazier.

Our precinct votes at the grade school I went to as a kid, which is about a half dozen blocks from where we live. When we arrived a little after seven thirty, there was Dodie Pembroke, with her baby in a papoose bag on her back, handing out Kieran cards. Already a line of people stretched from the front of the school clear around to the back where the voters went in. It kind of got me. Men, women, young ones, old ones, mothers carrying little kids. One guy was on crutches, another old fellow in a wheelchair. The day before, in American Government, Mr. Tyler had been talking about a free electorate and what happens when the people of a country either have no right to vote at all, or can vote only for communist or dictator-controlled candidates.

I waited down the street for about a half hour for my mother to come back from voting. She said, "What your father doesn't know doesn't hurt him—and I like that man Kieran."

I dropped her off at the store and then went to school but might as well have been somewhere else. All I could think about was how the voting was going. During lunch hour, I drove around to a couple of other voting places and there

129

were lineups at all of them. A noon-day broadcast on the radio said voting was the heaviest of any primary in years, but that it was anybody's guess how the vote might be going. I would have cut classes after that and driven down to headquarters, but I knew that Emily would give me the freeze if I did. I've never known anybody who had her hang-up on school. She could almost make me believe that getting an education was better than inheriting a million bucks. So I lasted it out, keeping an eye open for Quig to see if anything had happened while I was home sick. I didn't find him, though, and after school went down to headquarters.

I thought there'd be a big smash, the way there'd been the day before, but things were pretty quiet. Phone calls were still coming in from people who hadn't voted yet and needed a ride, and the minute I arrived Emily dispatched me to pick up a couple of old nuns at St. Meinhard's, the Catholic high school. I waited outside the synagogue, the polling place for their precinct, until they finally came tottering out.

After that, I called Emily from a nearby pay phone to find out where I was supposed to go next and she told me. It kept up like this until seven o'clock that night when I phoned in for what I hoped would be the last time.

"Oh, Douglas," Emily said. "I'm so glad it's you! I just don't think I would have dared ask anyone else. But this time we have a little different situation. This person who just called has her own car and can get to the polls all right, but she needs someone to stay with her children while she's gone and can't get a sitter." She paused, to let this sink in, then said, "Douglas, are you there?"

I took a deep breath and said I was.

130

"It won't be hard. The baby's already in bed and the other little boy can entertain himself. He's been sick or his mother would take him with her." She gave me the address and the woman's name and hung up before I could change my mind.

The baby turned out to be in bed, just the way Emily said, only she didn't say he was in bed crying—or that he had a pair of lungs like Tarzan. The other kid could entertain himself, too, as long as I was his horse.

Even so, the first half hour wasn't so bad. But by eight thirty, my knees were getting sore and the baby's crying was driving me up the wall. I went in the bedroom once to pick him up, but the smell drove me out.

Although the polls had closed at eight, by nine o'clock the kids' mother still wasn't home and I began to get desperate. Not only from the screaming, but because I didn't know how the election was going. There were two TV sets in the house, but on one all I could get was a snowstorm with no sound and on the other nothing at all. If there was a radio around the place, I couldn't find it.

I called headquarters about fifty times, but a lot of other people were doing the same thing and I never got through.

It was almost ten o'clock before the kids' mother came rolling in, smelling like a brewery. She said she'd had car trouble and hadn't got to vote after all which made the evening just about perfect.

In The Bomb I switched on the radio then turned it off. After I'd waited this long to hear how the election turned out, if Kieran had lost I didn't want to be by myself when I heard about it.

Even after I got to headquarters, I stood outside for a minute before going in. It looked as if everyone who'd ever

131

worked for Senator Kieran was there. As I squeezed in, I heard an exciting television voice announce, "Now to repeat. After see-sawing back and forth since the polls closed two hours ago, a winning pattern has been established that supports what the computers predicted more than an hour ago. . . ."

I didn't hear the rest. I didn't need to. Emily was working her way toward me through the crowd. I'd never seen her cry before and it just about killed me. Her face wasn't screwed up or anything, tears were just running down her cheeks. I put my arms around her and held her up against my chest. "It's all right," I said. I was too choked up myself to say anything more.

Then from someplace around my collar bone, this muffled voice said, "All right! Of course, it's all right! He's winning, you dumb crazy dope!"

★ ★ ★ ★ ★ ★

Chapter 11

☆ ☆ ☆ ☆ ☆ ☆

WE'D BEEN FIVE hours on the road and I still couldn't believe that I was skimming west on the Interstate—there was even a big, fat moon in the sky—with Emily beside me on the front seat. I'll admit that if Emily was crazy about me she didn't show it, and instead of sitting at the wheel of a Maserati traveling a cool hundred and twenty miles an hour, I was in The Bomb doing sixty-five. The difference, this was for real and the Maserati and the blonde with her hands in my hair was something I'd dreamed up.

I'd started thinking about going to California right after Kieran won in our primary. A week later when he won in Oregon, I couldn't get it out of my mind. I can't explain it, but I had to help him. From the day I brought that load of stuff to headquarters for Mr. Tyler the time his car wouldn't start, life had started changing for me. Most important, it had brought me Emily. But there were other things, too. Although as far as the yearbook was concerned, nothing had ever come of all the petitions the kids had signed—it was coming out, Quig said, with a cover just as stuffy as the year before—something had happened to *me*. I couldn't have slipped back into being nobody again if I'd tried. At school, I couldn't walk fifty feet down the corridor without some kid calling me by name. And most unbelievable of all, the day after the election Bernie Meyer had asked me to write a story for the last issue of the paper on student involvement in the Kieran campaign.

The only clunker in the whole affair was me making myself scarce after Curley's accident. So far, he hadn't talked. When he got out of the hospital he simply told police he didn't know the name of the guy he'd been dragging with. But that didn't mean he was going to keep quiet about it forever. Curley had his ways.

When I thought about that, I got sick inside. Not that I'd done anything so wrong, but I just couldn't bear to think of Emily finding out. It didn't help any that I hadn't wanted to drag, or that Curley had goaded me into it. *I* should have better sense. It didn't help that if Curley hadn't been high on pot his distance perception wouldn't have been all screwed up, and he probably wouldn't have run into the telephone pole—*I* knew he was smoking—or that if he hadn't been smoking, the diesel oil wouldn't have ignited and "Shad" wouldn't have got himself half-burned to death.

The truth was that I had contributed to the accident and had then run away from it.

A truck about a half block long sailed past on the left almost swallowing The Bomb in the undertow. Emily's head drooped down a bit on my shoulder and cramped my right arm a little, but I didn't mind. I wanted her to sleep as long as she could. When it was her turn to drive I planned to crawl into the back seat and really sack out. Laugh if you want to, but I'd done the same thing my dad

134

did when Norm and I were little and the family was taking a trip somewhere—put the suitcases and some boxes on the floor and a crib mattress on top of them so the width of the back seat was just about doubled. I'd tested it before we started, and although I couldn't even begin to stretch out, it was better than sleeping sitting up. The really crazy thing—though Emily didn't think so—was that my mother had kept the mattress all these years. I found it in the attic, wrapped in plastic, the folded up crib along side it.

It was figuring out a way to sleep and discovering that Emily could drive—though I should have known she could do most anything—that had made me decide that it might be possible for us to go to California and help Senator Kieran the last couple of days before the election, after all.

Until then, it had been completely hopeless. The plane fare for me alone—and I wasn't going without Emily, I knew that—was almost a hundred and eighty bucks, and my bank account was at an all-time low. And while I was confident that The Bomb could take us to California and back, I just didn't see how with me doing all the driving, we could get to Los Angeles, spend three or four days there helping Kieran and get back to Cedar City, without shooting the entire last week of school. And I didn't have that kind of time. I was still holding my breath about graduating. My name was on the list, all right, but even with Mr. Tyler, Miss Philbrick, and Steinfeld on my side—I'd had a talk with him a couple of weeks before and decided he was a pretty decent guy—it wouldn't take much to get my name off the list, either. I still had to pass a final exam in math which, out of pure cussedness, old Mayerling had put off giving.

135

Then one night when I was at headquarters helping Emily get things organized for our delegates who were going to the convention, just like that it hit me how it might be done.

"Listen," I said, "do you drive?"

". . . fifty-six, fifty-seven, fifty-eight," Emily said, counting support cards, "don't be silly. Of course, I drive."

"Well, then, listen some more," I said. "This is how we can do it. I'll fix up a place in The Bomb for us to take turns sleeping, and we drive straight through. We don't stop at all, except to get food, go to the john, and stretch our legs. Averaging sixty miles an hour—and The Bomb can do a lot better than that—we'll be in L.A. Saturday evening. We'll go to the Y, sack out until morning, then go to headquarters and see what they've got for us to do." I paused to see how Emily was taking all of this and when I saw she'd put down the stack of support cards and was kind of staring off into space, I went on. "We work all day Sunday, Monday, and Tuesday, stick around for the victory celebration that night—in L.A. it ought to be something—get some sleep and then start back to Cedar City on Wednesday. We get home sometime Thursday and I'm back in school on Friday."

"You'll miss four days of school," Emily said in this small, very final voice, "and you can't afford it."

It was a hare-brained scheme and in my heart I hadn't expected Emily to buy it. Even so, I didn't think she needed to sound so final about it. "Skip it," I said, sounding sore.

Emily didn't seem to have heard. "Actually, we wouldn't have to be there Tuesday at all. They'll have plenty of people working that last day. And while being there for the

136

victory celebration would be nice, it's not important. If we left Monday night, we'd be back in Cedar City in time for you to go to school Wednesday morning. Not that you'd be good for much, but you'd be there and that counts for something."

Although I knew Emily wanted to go every bit as much as I did, I still couldn't believe she was serious. But she was. Not completely, but enough so really to listen when I went out and got some sectional maps I had in the car and showed her that except for two not very long stretches we'd have the interstate, divided, or four-lane highways all the way.

Then Emily said we weren't realistic if we thought we could average sixty miles an hour, and that we had to be sensible. Fifty miles an hour, she said, was much more like it. But even at fifty, and allowing for longer breaks, she figured we could get to L.A. late Saturday night or early Sunday morning.

Now that we were actually on our way, however, I could see that in spite of a late start, we might do better than that. The number on the odometer turned over as I glanced at the dash. Four hundred and fifty miles in a little less than eight hours, and we'd stopped three times. Twice to get something to eat and once just to stretch our legs. Our late start was one of those things. At the last minute, I'd decided to stay after school and tell Mr. Tyler that Emily and I were going to California but that I'd be back in school on Wednesday. He said we were out of our minds—but he grinned when he said it—and for God's sake, to be careful. Then it took longer than I thought it would to write the note I was leaving for my mother. Emily had slowed us up some more. There'd been a crisis of some kind at headquarters so she was late getting home, and then we had to wait almost an hour to get a long-distance call through to her folks, to tell them she was going to California but not to worry.

I was doing a little calculating, figuring how much of our lost time we still had to make up, when Emily stirred beside me, then laughed softly.

"I guess I went to sleep."

"I guess you did," I said. "Snored, too."

"You can demand equal time," Emily said. "Right now, if you want. I really do feel rested."

I started to say I wasn't tired, but I yawned before I could finish the sentence.

"OK," Emily said. "That does it. Over to the side of the road, little buddy, and let me have the wheel."

I waited a while to see how she managed The Bomb and she did fine, so I piled into the back and it really wasn't bad. The funny thing, though, was that suddenly I wasn't sleepy any more. For one thing, it started getting light and it was just so damned pretty I hated to close my eyes. Although the sun wasn't up, there was this kind of wash in the sky so you could see the faint outlines of hills off in the distance. Before very long, the wash started getting pinker and pinker until it looked as if Somebody had taken this great big paintbrush and brought it in a big half circle right at the point where the earth meets the sky. Away in the distance I heard a meadowlark singing. It was a Western, whose song isn't like an Eastern meadowlark's at all and I remembered when Quig and I were kids and we used to flush them from a field when we were hiking.

Just then, the meadowlark let out another of those sweet,
138

gurgly calls and Emily said, real softly, "Listen, Doug. A Western."

"Yeah," I said. "A Western," and then this crazy thing happened. Maybe because I was really pretty tired, or maybe just because I was happy, for about thirty seconds I thought I was going to cry because she knew the difference.

I don't wake up very easily and it was a little while before I realized that Emily was leaning over me, shaking my shoulder and saying, "Doug, wake up." For a while I couldn't remember whether it was the second or the third time I'd crawled into the back for a nap. Then something brought me to real fast. The Bomb wasn't moving. It was standing still and the sun was sinking low in the sky.

"The Bomb was making this kind of a noise," Emily said. "Not bad. Just this kind of clunk and I thought you'd want to know."

"Yeah," I said. "Sure." Though I said it very cool, for my money, any kind of a noise in a car is bad. "Let's take a look."

Emily had pulled The Bomb onto the shoulder and raised the hood, but though I poked around, whatever was wrong I couldn't see it. I started the motor, took a listen, and what I heard wasn't good. But when you can't afford a tow, and we couldn't, there was nothing to do but go on.

All this while, Emily hadn't asked a lot of stupid questions about what did I think was wrong, and was it serious, and did I think I could fix it, which shows you almost better than anything what kind of a girl she really is.

The sun was lower still in the sky and the cars still whizzing by us on the highway when shimmering in the distance ahead of us was the first sign we'd seen in hours. "Pandora—4 miles."

If you've never been to Pandora, don't go. Though as Emily said, the people were nice. If they hadn't been, the two days and two nights we spent there would have been even worse than they were. The woman who runs the creamery let Emily sleep in her spare bedroom and after Mr. Poynter, who had a sort of combination garage and hardware store, got home from his fishing trip Sunday night, he put me up on a cot on his front porch.

It was Monday, though, before he started working on The Bomb and even then rebuilding a generator takes some doing. Though I know pretty much about cars, I couldn't have done it in a week. Yet by Monday night, The Bomb was not only running, but for an old girl, sounded pretty good. I'd pumped gas for Mr. Poynter while he worked on The Bomb—you'd really be surprised at how many cars came off the interstate to fill up at his pump—so that brought the price of the repair job down some. And while Emily didn't get paid for helping the creamery lady, she fed us free so we weren't out of pocket for that. Even so, I had less than twenty bucks in my wallet and instead of heading west, we were going back to Cedar City.

Emily had been crying, though she'd done her best to hide it, I could tell.

We got a good start Monday night and by mid-morning Tuesday we were halfway home. We didn't talk a lot, we both felt too bad. We'd tried to get to California to help Kieran and we hadn't made it, that was all. Neither of us was so dumb that we thought Kieran would win or lose in California because of us. What we both did know was that if Kieran lost in California—there Frazier, not Swallow, was the chief contender—there was no hope for him at all at the national convention. Kieran had said as much, himself. In fact, some people had criticized him for it, saying that he was a self-defeatist. But as Emily said, this only made her like him more. That a time had come for honesty, not only in politics, but in a politician's personal life, as well.

About five o'clock Tuesday afternoon we took a short rest stop, gassed The Bomb then moved on. We'd decided earlier that about eleven o'clock that night—with the difference in time we had no hope of hearing any significant returns before then—we'd take a real break. Eat a good meal and listens to the returns.

As it turned out, it was almost midnight before we stopped but that was all right. The restaurant was pretty much like all the others along the way. A long, low building located as close to the exit as it could be placed, a gift shop, a couple of gas pumps, and no matter what hour of the day or night, a lot of cars and trucks parked out in front.

This place wasn't that busy, but still we had to wait a while before a waitress took our order and we could ask if they had a television set we could watch for a while. She said they used to have one, but people hung around and watched it after they'd finished eating so they got rid of it.

That got rid of Emily and me, too. As hungry as we were, we decided to go on. By then, the California polls had been closed for more than two hours and so far all we'd learned over the radio in The Bomb was that the voting was heavy and that this precinct or that, had gone to Governor Frazier or Senator Kieran.

We knew little more than that when we stopped again.

Emily looked pale as I opened the car door and her hand was cold in mine as we walked toward the door of the restaurant. "TV aerials," she said.

I had seen them, too, and I held her hand a little tighter. The place was not as crowded as the one we'd been before, but even at that hour it seemed noisy and cheerful. In spite of the aerials, however, there was no TV set in sight. "We still have to eat," I said. "Let's sit down."

"Find out first," Emily said. "I'll wait here."

"Pardon me," I said to the waitress behind the lunch counter, "is there a TV set we can watch while we eat?"

"Cocktail lounge. Through that door and to your right." She put down a cup of coffee and a fried egg sandwich in front of a customer, then looked up sharply. "No minors, though, it's the law." She had a lot of red hair done up in a net and a hard, sharp face. She moved off down the counter to a coffee machine and I followed her. "Listen," I said. "Please. I don't want a drink. Neither does my girl. We just want to eat and find out how the election is coming out, that's all."

She didn't look up from the pie she was cutting. "Kieran?"

"Who else?" I said. I had to take a chance.

"Well, then, what are you waiting for? *I* don't have eyes in the back of my head. Get your food and take it in there. You're big enough to be of legal age even if you're not, and if you're not married to that peaked little thing over there by the door you ought to be ashamed of yourself."

The lounge was nice. Just dark enough and no one else was there. We pulled two chairs together and ate our food.
142

The old girl must have fixed our hamburgers herself or had some words with the cook, because they were fat and juicy and were served with all the french fries we could eat. I guess you could say it was about the closest thing to a real date I'd ever had with Emily.

From time to time we'd switch from one network to another, and though no one was ready to project results, it seemed to us that little by little Kieran's margin over Frazier was growing.

Happiness isn't something you can describe and I won't try. But sitting there with Emily, knowing that there were all those thousands and thousands of people in California who felt the way we did about Kieran, and if we and enough other people like us worked our tails off he might be President of the United States, well, I could have died of it.

When the figures started to change and go the other way we weren't concerned. They had swung back and forth from the very beginning. Then it happened. The voice of an announcer increased in pitch as his face increased in size on the screen. "On the basis of computerized projections Governor Frazier is the winner. Governor Frazier has forty-six percent of the vote, Senator Kieran forty-four percent, and the former Senator Swallow ten percent. Let me repeat . . ."

I got up and switched the station but I couldn't change the results. But even then we didn't believe it.

"Computers make mistakes," I said.

"All the time," Emily said bravely, then suddenly she seemed to shrink beside me. "This is the end of everything."

"It doesn't have to be the end," I spoke roughly. "On paper, maybe, this gives Frazier enough votes to get the nomina-

143

tion, but something can still happen at the convention." I was trying to convince myself as well as her.

Emily shook her head. "The party wants someone it can control. They can't control Kieran."

"Maybe four years from now . . ." I put my arm around her shoulders.

"In four years anything can happen." She'd started to cry soundlessly. "In four years . . . you may be dead. No . . . No . . . I don't mean that. Just hold me, Doug, hold me for a minute very close."

The waitress with the red hair came in and took away our dishes. "Sorry, kids," she said softly, and went out.

Less than ten minutes later we were on our way again.

★ ★ ★ ★ ★ ★

Chapter 12

☆ ☆ ☆ ☆ ☆ ☆

IF YOU THINK things can't get any worse than they already are, you're wrong. They can.

As I got to the top of the stairs my mother said, "Dougie, is that you?"

The door to her bedroom was open and as my eyes got used to the dark I could see that she wasn't in bed but sitting in her little rocking chair by the window. I hoped she hadn't been sitting there waiting for me ever since I'd left on Friday, but that didn't seem to be on her mind at all. Maybe she was just glad to have me back, though I don't know why.

"You can turn on the light," she said. "That little one on the dresser."

When I did, I could see that she hadn't undressed and that she had cried until her face was swollen. Then in that kind of crazy way you notice something crazy, I saw she hadn't put her hair up on her rollers. That's why, when she said, "It's Norm," I thought he was dead.

"You haven't heard. It was on the news . . . in the paper . . ."

145

"Does Dad know?" It was all I could think to say.

My mother nodded, caught her breath. "He called from Omaha. He heard it there. He won't do anything . . . he said Norm got himself into this thing and he'll have to get himself out."

It took me about a minute to comprehend. If Norm had got himself into something and had to get himself out, he wasn't dead.

"No bail . . . no lawyer . . . nothing."

Then I got it. If Norm needed bail he was in jail. "OK, what has he done this time? Killed somebody?" Suddenly, I was mad all over. Not only because I'd had the pants scared off of me, but because Norm was such a damned fool.

"And I was worried about you, too," Mom said, and started blubbering again. So I added myself to the damned fool list and tried to get my mother calmed down enough to find out what happened.

It took fifteen minutes to find out that the first she'd heard had been at work when a customer told her they were having trouble at the university again. Graduation exercises had been interrupted by heckling students who took over the microphone and scattered the diplomas. Police had been called.

My mother worried all afternoon that Norm might have been in on it, but it wasn't until she got home and saw the evening paper that she learned the worst. While the graduation exercises had been going on, or rather, *not* going on, Norm and two other students had broken into one of the university offices, jammed the IBM machines that handled the university salary checks and hauled five boxes of records out into the courtyard and burned them.

146

"There's a picture in the paper," my mother said, and started bawling again.

I picked the paper up from the floor and it was like she said. On the front page was a picture of a big bonfire and Norm and another guy getting ready to heave another box of papers on it. A cop had Norm by the arm, and in the background a fireman was dragging up a hose.

"It was on the TV news, too," my mother said, trying not to cry, "and they had this close-up view of Norm. He . . . he looks bad. I could tell. He hasn't been taking care of himself."

"Oh, my God," I said, but not loud enough for her to hear.

"Someone asked him why he did it, and he said he was standing on his constitutional rights and was going to plead the fifth amendment. But they arrested him just the same."

With that, the flood started all over again so I went down to the kitchen and made a pot of coffee and brought it upstairs to her. I was leaving to go to bed myself, though it hardly seemed worth it for only two hours sleep, when she stopped me.

"Oh, I almost forgot. You had a phone call. It was a girl. She said her name was Sherlie Lou. She said Curley was ready to talk and that he'd be getting in touch with you." My mother looked at me anxiously and she sounded as if she was getting ready to cry all over again. "Douglas, I didn't know that you knew any—Sherlie Lous. . . ."

"Don't worry about that," I said. "Everything is going to be all right."

I figured I owed her that lie, though I knew that for me nothing would ever be all right again. That call from Sherlie

147

Lou mean only one thing. Blackmail. I wondered how much it would be and how long I could pay it. Maybe until after Emily went back to New Hampshire. Then, at least she wouldn't know.

Right after school, I went home and read the paper which I hadn't had time to look at that morning. The main story on page one was about Kieran's defeat in California.

A news analysis said that the Chicago convention would now be a ho-hum affair, with Frazier probably getting the nomination on the second ballot. I couldn't bear to read any more. Kieran, after publicly congratulating Frazier had left for an undisclosed destination to get some rest.

The story about Norm and the trouble at the university had been moved to an inside page, but there was a lot of it. Norm, himself, was still in jail and had gone on a hunger strike. The Student Committee for Academic Freedom, which was an off-shoot of an off-shoot of SDS, was trying to raise bail to get him out. The whole thing made my heart hurt to think about it. I left a note for my mother, who'd gone to work that morning though she shouldn't have, saying not to call me for dinner; that I was going to bed and sack out until seven o'clock the next morning.

But it was a long time before I could turn off my mind. How could Norm destroy property and deny the rights of others and still demand "rights" from a Constitution that he said was outworn and should be discarded? I remembered what Watt Tyler had once said in class about the difference between disagreement and dissent. He said he'd heard it in college from a teacher named Dan Boorstin, and he made us write down that disagreement produces debate, but dissent produces dissension; that people who disagree have an argument, but people who dissent have a quarrel; and that
148

disagreement is the life blood of democracy, and dissension is its cancer.

Maybe that was what was wrong with our world. And now we didn't have Gregory Kieran to help find a cure.

I talked to Emily a couple of times during the next few days but I didn't see her. She was busy at headquarters again, helping get things ready for the convention though now no one had any heart for it. She said that the day after California primary the kids who'd come down to headquarters had worn black arm bands, but Red Beard had made them take them off. He said we couldn't let down until the convention, itself, was over.

On Saturday, early, I got a call from the cement plant I'd worked for the summer before saying they had a day's work for me so I took it. I'd be needing the money.

The second call had come right after I got home from school on Friday and the minute I heard the cheap, tinny voice I knew it was Sherlie Lou.

She said Curley had gone out of town for a few days to look at a car he thought he might buy and that as I was kind of responsible for the diesel being burned up, he thought I might like to help him pay for the new car. A little something every couple of weeks or so.

I wanted to hang up but was afraid. And I couldn't have if I tried. My hand was frozen to the receiver. I said I'd talk to Curley about it when he got back and broke the connection when Sherlie started cussing. The only good thing about the conversation was that my mother wasn't home. Sherlie Lou's voice didn't need any amplifier. With earmuffs, you could have heard her in the next room.

I worked overtime on Saturday, and by the time I got

149

down to headquarters that night it was almost nine o'clock.

The place was dark. I got the key and opened up, thinkabout all the other Saturday nights, week-nights, even, when people were down there working and how happy we all had been knowing that we were working for something important. Now, even though I'd done all right on the math test and my name was still on the graduating list, I felt vacant inside. Soon Emily would be going away and I'd go off to the Army. Before, when I'd thought about the Army I'd sustained myself by thinking about what I was going to do afterwards. But now, going to South America or Alaska or wherever didn't appeal to me so much. I even had this crazy notion that I might look into that junior college my father said catered to the "whole" student, wondering if they'd consider a "half" student like me. Going to college was better than not looking forward to anything at all.

I was sitting at Emily's desk when this strange thing happened. This parade of people began to march slowly through the room. I could see them as plainly as if they were there. There was Red Beard and Dodie, with her baby in the papoose carrier on her back. Joe and Molly, Mike Bridges, the fat boy and Betty Stringfellow. Mrs. P, who'd licked a thousand stamps and addressed as many envelopes came next, with D'Mario and Gribbles just behind. It hadn't been too long ago that I'd thought all blacks were either Panthers or shiftless. Now I knew that Gribbles' father was dead and he was helping support his mother and a bunch of younger brothers and sisters. (He was a *black* Quig—or maybe it was the other way around.) Behind him were more kids, black and white, square and kooky, plain and Panther, who'd

150

stopped in at headquarters on their way home from Tech High and emptied their pockets of change in the campaign bucket by the door; kids from all over the city were behind them—kids who had worked and believed in the Senator.

Though the night was hot for June and the door propped open for a bit of breeze, I felt goose bumps creep along my arms. Watt Tyler had appeared to wind up the parade. Then I had to grin at my fancy. He was real.

He said, "Hi, Doug," then wanted to know if I'd heard about Quig getting a Merit Scholarship, and I said I had —that it was the only good thing I had heard all day. He asked me how things were with Norm.

I pulled myself together and said I guessed all right. That the SCAF had raised the money and Norm was out of jail. After that, Mr. Tyler sort of milled around the room but pretty soon he came back to stand beside me. I'd never seen him look so serious before, and when he spoke it was slowly, as if he was measuring every word.

"I came down here tonight hoping that just being in the place would help me make up my mind. And it has. So I guess you'll be the first to know. I'm going to stick my neck out, stick it way out and run for office."

I'd had my feet up on the desk and I put them down. Mr. Tyler running for office! I know it sounds crazy, but my heart started beating faster. It would be great to have him as Governor, or in Washington as Senator, or representative from our district. He probably wouldn't want to start out at the top—Lieutenant Governor, maybe. I couldn't think what else good there was.

Mr. Tyler, who'd started wandering around again and seemed to have forgotten all about me, paused under this

151

big picture of Kieran that was thumbtacked to the wall. "The Board of County Commissioners, I think, is the place where I'll begin." Then he nodded, as if the picture on the wall had answered him. "There's no better place to start than the third district, which is my own back yard."

The county! I couldn't believe it. I didn't even know for sure how many county commissioners there were, or even what they did. I was as dumb about county politics as I'd been about national politics a few months before. And that was pretty dumb. Whatever Mr. Tyler wanted, though, was all right with me.

Mr. Tyler had turned from the picture and was facing me. "But I'm going to need all the help I can get, Doug. People in my district have been voting for Wiley Asphalter for so long they don't even look to see if there's anybody else on the ticket. I won't have Gabby to help on this one. He's got a project of his own he's working on. Pretty soon Emily will be leaving, so I'm going to have to depend a lot on you."

"Anything I can do." I had trouble getting the words out because there seemed to be a golf ball stuck in my throat.

"Drop by and see me when you've got time—at home or at school, I'll be teaching part of the summer—and we'll map out some strategy. In the meantime, keep it to yourself —tell Emily, of course—until I decide the right time to announce."

I said I would and went to the door with him, watched as he walked a ways down the street to where his car was parked. It didn't seem to start much better, I noticed, in June than it did when it was cold. But instead of getting a new car, Watt Tyler would be spending the money on a political
152

campaign, with no other purpose than to help make Cedar City and Watson County a better place to live in. I got that tight feeling in my throat again and had to blow my nose.

There was a county map in one of the drawers in Red Beard's desk showing the different districts marked in red. This third district, the one Mr. Tyler wanted to represent, was a big one. Shaped rather like a fat upside-down letter "L," it took in most of the west side where Mr. Tyler lived, continued south for a long way until it crossed the railroad tracks, turned left where there was a big wooded area that people said should be made into a park, crossed more tracks and wound up at city dump and sewage disposal plant. I began to see that Mr. Tyler would have a lot of work to do. And he wanted me to help him. *Me.* It gave me a funny feeling. Would he still want me to help him if he knew I'd been the one dragging with Curley the night of the accident? The one who'd been too chicken to admit it?

I don't know how long I sat there thinking. Five minutes, ten minutes, longer—I don't know—before I went into one of the back offices and picked up the phone book. I'd read in the paper that "Shad" was home for a few days before being flown to some big burn center in Dallas for further treatment.

There was a lot of Morrisons in the phone book but only two J.M.'s. The first one I hit it wrong, but on the second when I asked if Police Officer Morrison could come to the phone the man who answered said, "This is he." Like an English teacher, for God's sake.

I said, "This is Doug Radigan," then I got pretty incoherent. But I did get it all out. I mean, about being sorry, and that I was the one who had been dragging with Curley

153

and who had, in a way, been responsible for everything that happened.

"I'm glad you called," said "Shad," "though, of course, I had a pretty good idea it was you."

"You did?" I guess I gave myself away with that, and then "Shad" laughed.

"Who else? Cops aren't really as dumb as you think."

"But you didn't tell . . ." I was still pretty aghast.

"Cops don't tell everything they know," he said, "in spite of what you may think. And even if they did, what you did wasn't a federal offense. You can't be charged for it."

I made kind of a long, wheezing sound into the receiver and "Shad" laughed again. "So forget it."

"Curley can't get me in trouble?"

I got another laugh for that.

"Well, thanks," I said. "Thanks for everything." I hung up because I was afraid I might start blubbering.

I went back to Red Beard's desk and put my head down on my arms and took a couple of big, deep breaths. When I looked up Emily was coming in the door.

"Mr. Tyler is going to run for county commissioner from this district," I said, pointing with a finger at the map. "He left here just a little while ago. He said I could tell you, but no one else."

Emily clasped her hands in front of her as if she was saying a little prayer and squeezed her eyes tightly shut. Tears leaked out and tangled in her eyelashes. She was smiling. "I just can't believe it . . . that he would be so brave . . ."

"I know. But he said that's the place to begin—right in his own back yard. But he's going to need help though. All

154

he can get." Even with Emily so near me, I couldn't get my mind off all the things that were going to have to be done before we got Mr. Tyler elected.

"I could stay on for a while," Emily said, taking my handkerchief to blow her nose. "Maybe all summer—now that there's something important for me to do."

It took a second for what she'd said to sink in, and when it did I swung Emily clear off her feet.

"Douglas!" she squealed, the way girls do but that Emily never had before.

I couldn't help laughing I was so happy.

"Put me down and I'll tell you something."

"Tell me first.'"

"I can't. I can't think properly unless you put me down."

I put her down. "What is it?"

Emily's cheeks were pink. "Maybe you won't believe it, but Mr. Tyler going into politics is like an omen. Maybe you won't believe it, but that's what I've been thinking you should do when you're out of college. Of course, you'll have to study very hard. And read, read, read . . ."

"Me," I said. "You mean, *me* run for something?"

Emily laughed. "Why not? It's a big country. Any number can play, and there are lots of jobs." Suddenly, she was sober. "There isn't anything better for young people to do than get involved in politics. Thomas Jefferson, you know, was only twenty-six when he was elected to the House of Burgesses from Virginia . . ."

"Mr. Tyler's twenty-six."

"I know. And Thomas Jefferson was only twenty-nine when he wrote the Declaration of Independence."

Emily's eyes were shining.

155

I put my arms around her and she didn't move away.

"Oh, Emily," I whispered. "Radigan cares, Radigan cares a lot."

"So does Emily," she whispered back, and I held her closer still.

Then suddenly I could see myself speaking before this big crowd of people. There were kids, old people, blacks and whites. Banners everywhere spelled out RADIGAN. I couldn't tell what I was running for; it didn't matter. I had something I'd never had before—a future.

With people like Mr. Tyler running for office—and Emily and me and all kids everywhere doing everything they could to help—so did our country.